AMERICAN NONSENSICAL

ALSO BY EDWARD D. WEBSTER

FICTION

The Gentle Bomber's Melody (2013)

Soul of Toledo (2016)

Carlos Crosses the Line, A Tale of Immigration,
Temptation and Betrayal in the Sixties (2020)

NON-FICTION

A Year of Sundays, Taking the Plunge and our Cat
to Explore Europe (2004)

AMERICAN NONSENSICAL

A Farce, Both Tragic and True

Edward D. Webster

Casa de los Sueños Publishing

To sensible people and those who try to be

CHAPTER 1

JEFF

June 2001, Naomi, Nebraska

Jeff was going nuts; no doubt about it. Still, he had to perform. He owed it to his mom, to the people who were coming to see him, and to Jesus. His mom cherished him. She'd given him life and taught him so much, initiated their *holy mission* and made him a star. She'd given him Ruby! If he made it through tonight, he'd have a few days to rest. He *could* do this!

The gathering turned out to be puny, not much over 100, under a circus tent in an open field. Rain beat down on the canvas overhead. Soothing. Hypnotic. Ominous.

A recording blared over the speakers, *When the Saints Go Marching In.* —Pretty freakin' funny.

Jeff wore his white suit, white tie, pale blue shirt; clothes to inspire wonder. His mom floated ahead of him, up the stairs, radiant in her blond hair and flowing white gown. The spotlight lit her up. Fans blasted streams of air, sending her gown billowing.

Jeff forced a smile and stepped onstage. He and his mom raised their gloved hands over their heads. The crowd applauded. He reached for the microphone stand and tilted it toward him.

"Good evening, I'm Jeff Lamb, and this is my momma, Sarah." He hated calling her *momma*, but she insisted. *It fits our image, son.*

The crowd bellowed their approval. Jeff stepped aside, and his mother took over. "My son and I, we come to share a glorious story."

She always began that way. The story would commence with Jesus, and move on to the *gift* the Lord had bestowed on Jeff. His mother's phony, buoyant voice disgusted him tonight. Not the first time. Jeff tuned it out and scanned the audience; women in long, flowered dresses, men in their best shirts, some wearing bolo ties.

As always, there were the few by the front with canes or crutches; rounded up by their *program organizer*, Bob Smithfield; waiting to be *healed*. Smithfield's helpers would be out among the crowd now, *collecting for God's work*. Jeff recognized a couple of the invalids, who'd been *healed* at one of their previous revivals, maybe last week in Kansas City. They'd switched maladies. The wheelchair guy from last time was on crutches tonight, and he wore a fake beard. The lame woman, newly blind, wore dark glasses and carried a white cane.

Front and center in the audience, a blond girl. Jeff's heartbeat kicked up until he saw that it wasn't Suzi.

Once he'd felt superior to these people. He thought they'd all come to worship him. But how many came just to gawk at a freak of nature?

His mother was clever or evil. Jeff was superior or even holy, as she'd told him, or just another charlatan. "It doesn't matter how we convince them," she'd said. "We bring them to the Lord, and He saves them."

He didn't feel clever or holy tonight. He felt vile as fresh cow plop.

If he could have slept last night, if those nagging doubts had let him slumber any night the past week, this would feel so different. If he could truly heal one doubting sinner, his faith could carry him through. Maybe tonight.

It was hot onstage. Faces in the audience grew blurry. The not-Suzi was pretty. She zeroed in on him. Did this one think he could impregnate her with a tear drop?

Buzzing filled his ears. His hands trembled. Sweat ran down his face and soaked the back of his shirt. This happened sometimes. Nothing to worry about. Nerves. All part of the act, except it wasn't; it was part of Jeff melting down. He could fight it like always. He could!

"I know what you want to see," his mother intoned. "You want to see the miracle hands of Christ."

Jeff looked at his hands, one and then the other, half expecting to see crimson splotches staining the palms of his white cotton gloves.

"For God has given us the miracle of Jeff's healing hands," she said. "The Lord never lets us down."

The people below stared at him, waiting.

"Behold," she said. "The holy spirit enters our presence." He knew she was directing the audience to him with outstretched arms, but the buzzing ground away Jeff's will. He was supposed to rise up on his toes, hands stretching toward heaven. He was supposed to imbue his features with heavenly joy and reach out to the audience as the spotlight narrowed on his angelic face. He was supposed to take the microphone and announce that those he touched would be saved.

The spotlight illuminated only his doubts. The people stared, wanting the carnival act that was Jeff Lamb, the magnificent, the Messiah's chosen.

Too shaken to face the spotlight, too paralyzed to produce a beatific smile, too feeble to raise his hands and bless those poor sinners, Jeff glanced down at the people, looking from face to face, casting about for anything that might energize him.

His mother came and touched his arm, shouting to the crowd, "What a blessing tonight, ladies and gentlemen. God's presence overwhelms Jeff. He will lift us up."

Blood, pulsing in his ears, set her voice warbling, merged with the buzzing, now an octave higher. That had never happened before. Her voice distorted to an undulating whine. "Holy rapture be upon us all."

Jeff Lamb was prime exhibit in this crazy deception his mother called, "Bringing Christ to the ignorant masses." He had to fight the droning in his head, to raise his hands high, to speak to the crowd and then go down and touch the invalids. Instead, his legs gave way. He dropped to the stage. He let his mother down.

CHAPTER 2

THIRTEEN YEARS EARLIER, SUMMER 1988, RURAL OKLAHOMA

Jeff ran out of the house, screen door slamming behind him. His mother shouted, "Jeffrey Little, you get back here."

She'd been explaining about Jesus again. He didn't understand how this story could be so important that she repeated over and over. This was *real* his mother said, not like television cartoons. This story was *holy*. Cartoons had good guys and bad guys and talking rabbits.

Jesus came in a book, instead of on TV. He talked lots about being good.

Jeff headed toward the vegetable garden where he could hide among the corn stalks. He looked back over his shoulder as he ran. His mother held the screen door open with one hand, her book, the bible, in the other. She wouldn't hit him with the book, it was *sacred*. She'd spank him with her open hand.

OHHHH. He tripped and went down, dirt smacking him in the face. A bolt of pain shot from his right hand. Something stuck out of the back of it. Jeff screamed and began bawling. It hurt awful, like nothing he'd ever felt.

Holy God—he'd landed on the little rake-thing his mother used to dig up dirt by the green beans. One of the four points ran right through from the palm to the back of his hand. Blood seeping around it.

Tears ran down his face. He stood and held it up, with the rake-handle dangling, toward his momma. She came running and then stopped short. She set the bible gently on the ground. She was crying too, staring hard at him. "It's okay. Hold still now." She grabbed his wrist with one hand and the rake-thing with the other and yanked him loose.

He screamed again and almost went out. She sat him on the ground and took off her apron. Blood ran fast from the wound. She was going to yell at him, call him, "bad boy," tell him God was punishing him for disobedience. He knew it. But her angry look disappeared. She smiled, as she squatted there, wrapping her apron tight around his hand, squeezing so it hurt even more.

She uncovered it again and examined it. "Good," she said. "This is very, very good, Jeff." She rewrapped it and tied her apron strings around.

Then she did something even stranger. She poked her finger into the blood that had fallen on the ground, raised her hand toward heaven and called out, "Thank you, Lord, for this blessing."

She helped Jeff up and walked him toward the house. "Now you have something in common with Jesus. Our Lord's hands and his feet were pierced by evil men. Come inside, and I'll tell you all about it."

JEFF'S WOUNDED RIGHT HAND oozed blood and puss for days, but his mother said they didn't need to go to the doctor. "God will heal you, if that's what He thinks best." Jeff didn't know why God would care about one little boy's hand, and what if He didn't think it best? Still, above all, Jeff trusted his momma to do the right thing.

His palm and the back of his hand itched like mad. When he scratched, clear fluid dripped from the palm. Sometimes it bled. After a while, the back of his hand began to scar up and the palm stopped oozing, but it still prickled something fierce. He gritted his teeth and fought the urge to gouge it with the jack knife he'd hidden in the garage.

Sometimes in the evening his momma handed him one of her knitting needles. "Poke it a little, honey. It'll feel better." He cried that first time, but he came to savor the feel—the persistent itch; the biting pain of the needle that somehow relieved it; the way the bleeding seemed to make her happy. She'd hug him then, whisper, "I love you," in his ear, and give him ice cream; chocolate-almond with fudge and whipped cream on top.

CHAPTER 3

THE BODY

October 2020, Outside Crownpoint, New Mexico

Northwest of Grants, New Mexico, uranium deposits stretch far and wide beneath the mesas and desolate countryside. Open pit mines there produced the bulk of America's uranium since the fifties. Core holes were drilled seeking new veins, shafts sunk, uranium extracted in quantities small or large. Nuclear disasters and near disasters tainted the industry. Demand dried up. Most mines were abandoned. Small operators walked away leaving a hazardous collection of open pits and mounds of toxic tailings. At the bottom of one of those pits, below a chalky-rock mesa, near Navajo land, lay the body. Like some ancient pharaoh, bound for the afterlife, artifacts surrounded it, including a well-thumbed bible.

Dead, like the pharaoh? Or alive? That was the question. The ultimate answer seemed inevitable.

CHAPTER 4

BUD

OCTOBER 2020, MANHATTAN BEACH CA

Whatever Stan tells you, he and I have a great partnership. He's the straight-arrow who plows ahead and gets things done. I think outside the box and find solutions. Stan's the handsome one—black hair, strong features, blue eyes. Not quite the type to play a doctor on TV, but, maybe, if he didn't shave compulsively. I'm the shorter, balding one, with a *Celtic complexion*. Our business is investigating fraud, a fancy way of saying we catch disability insurance cheats. Other types of cases when we can find the business. I shine at investigations. My skepticism is brilliant. When a guy's mother says, "Haven't seen him in months," I'm dying to barge into the back room and catch the guy ogling porn on his computer. My garage is full of pandemic Lysol and toilet paper. Now that's foresight.

I dig *conspiracy theories*, because not all theories are BS. Ask Einstein. By the way, I hear he's still alive down in Bolivia having mai-tais with Elvis.

Did Oswald kill JFK by himself? Don't know. Politicians cover things up. "In the interest of national security," they say. "For the good of the people." Yeah, sure.

Is there a Deep State? Absolutely.

As for Q-Anon, okay, some of it is wacko, but there's plenty of truth that no one knows for sure. Was Obama born in Hawaii or maybe Kenya? Is the earth flat? Some folks still claim that. –Wackos. Anti-vaxxers? –Sorry; I take my flu shot every October.

All of this nonsensical jive has come to a head between Stan and me over our amazing president. Donald Trump is my guy. He may not be doing TV shows any more, but he's the entertainer in chief. When he thinks something, he says it. A weird rumor; he passes it along. He launches little bits of his genius into the world along with some stuff that's pretty fucked up. True or not, he acts like what he's said is right, which makes him like lots of other *schmucks* in the world. That's one of the things I like about Trump. We're all *schmucks* in our own way, and our president isn't ashamed to act the part.

Which brings me to our problem: Stan and I have a *Donald Issue*. My partner and I used to joke all the time. We'd talk sports, argue over which drive-thru to stop at for lunch, but mostly we'd dissect the nonsense in Washington and Sacramento. Since Trump took over, Stan has clammed up. Sore loser? — It runs deeper than that.

Stan may not want to hear this, but here it is: our president might not always tell the truth, but he's strong, when most politicians are squishy as pig shit. He calls out the politically correct nonsense, like calling the illegals, *undocumented*. He stands up to our so-called allies and tells them to pay their share. A ball buster; that's what we need in a president. And this I can guarantee: when push comes to shove, Trump will do the right thing for America.

STAN

LET ME MAKE one thing clear: I love Bud, but he is *not* my business partner. The name on the door is S. Stein Investigations. S. is for Stanley, not Buddly.

Second, Bud's given name is Andy Randolph. Andy is a great name, but Bud rejects it.

Cheryl is my ex. When she and I divorced, she got the condo and half the investments. I received the rest of our holdings and the condo mortgage. To balance the scales, she passed on a priceless asset: Cheryl's brother, Bud. He was my friend before I knew her. He's a good guy, and he'd lost another job, so I hired him. But Bud can go off the deep end.

Bud and I disagree about lots of stuff. Take seatbelts. He wanted to disconnect the beeper in my Ford Escape so he could go strapless in peace. I stood up for safety and for avoiding a lawsuit that could bankrupt me after an accident. I believe in following the rules. Bud goes with, *f- - - authority.* That's another issue: Bud swears too much.

Now there's Covid-19. Bud thinks masks are for sissies, which are Democrats by default. The president of the US, whom Bud admires beyond reason, decided that masks were a joke. Bud followed suit. So did lots of our fellow Americans—some insane code of insolence. Deadly.

Back in our Army days, Bud and I joked about politics and about the Army brass. Politicians were our favorite *whores*—Bud's word not mine. Take guns: if people in a congressman's district wanted to do target practice on baby rabbits with AK47s, the local politico delivered righteous speeches about the Bill of Rights, no matter that it makes no sense. Funny or tragic? To remain sane sometimes you've got to laugh.

Now, Bud says I've lost my sense of humor. Maybe. I can joke about lots of stuff, but not Trump. When he mocks people who wear masks, it costs lives. When he pretends our elections are fixed, he denigrates our democracy. Bud and I tried to joke our way through it, but this is not funny. It threatens our friendship, and that breaks my heart.

CHAPTER 5

STAN

OCTOBER 2020

I climbed behind the wheel in the Escape, wearing my mask to protect Bud and me from each other's viral exhalations. Bud sat in the back as I insisted. As I drove, I saw him in my rearview mirror dangling his mask in the air like a cat with a toy. "This is such bull shit. I don't have the virus. If one of us got it, no big deal."

Tell that to the dead people, I thought. *Tell the ones who haven't recovered after six months.* He knew what I thought. I blew him a kiss, and he flipped me off.

Bud, still looking mischievous— "I found something momentous on the internet, Stan. Life changing."

"True or one of your famous gobs of BS?"

"From a professor of oral medicine."

"What if I don't want to hear it?"

"This professor posted a clip on YouTube. A really handsome fella in a white smock. He points out that brushing your teeth is detrimental."

"Thanks for that, Bud. Glad you're in back."

"Once or twice a month will keep the bacteria in your mouth at the optimal level. Brushing too much wears your teeth down. So, unless you want to turn your choppers to nubs …"

Hard to tell if Bud believed the stuff he dished up. "Was this doctor licensed?"

We were headed to surveil a guy who used to work at an Amazon warehouse, hurt on the job, he claimed. Bud had his camera ready to record video of him dancing an Irish jig, or lifting his car off the ground with one hand. Not uplifting work, but it paid our bills.

"A genuine oral surgeon," Bud said. "And he'd really thought this out. All his human patients who'd needed tooth extractions brushed every day."

"*Human* patients?" I asked. "He's what, an alien from outer space?" I looked in the mirror and spotted Bud's dopey grin.

"No way. I know what *Martians* look like."

"A veterinarian then?"

"Yeah, maybe. That doesn't mean he's wrong."

My cell phone buzzed. The green *Answer* and red *Decline* appeared on the dashboard along with the name, *Hannah Christian*. My heart beat a little faster. I reached toward the screen, but Bud launched himself from the back seat and grabbed my arm.

"Don't."

I hit *Decline*. "What the heck?"

"Someone I used to know," he said.

Which made me curious. "I know her too."

I pulled to the curb by a fire hydrant and turned in the seat. "You gotta tell me, Bud."

"No, I don't." After a minute he said, "She did something that fucked me up." Another few seconds and he added, "She's a beautiful bitch."

"She was my girlfriend once," I said.

Maybe, if I thought about it, she hadn't been that nice to me either.

I'D FALLEN FOR HANNAH in high school, when she was a cheerleader and I was a minor star on the soccer team. We dated all through senior year, danced through the prom together. The perfect couple; that's what I thought. She was so attractive, so adventuresome, so fun. I couldn't believe she'd fallen for me. I pictured myself marrying her one day.

Instead, we went off to separate colleges that freshman year. She shacked up with a sophomore over Thanksgiving instead of coming home to me. The special Thanksgiving reunion we'd planned, "with all the trimmings," Hannah had promised, went down the tubes. To me *the trimmings* had meant more than turkey and stuffing. I turned out to be the turkey, roasted, stuffed, deflated and more miserable than I'd ever thought possible.

Later she asked me to forgive her. —Not in my make-up. Her mother died that year. Hannah called, and I hung up on her. Later, I found out she'd attempted suicide. I tried telling myself it wasn't my fault but never quite believed it.

Fast forward twenty years. I met her at our reunion last June, just as sexy and just as shapely as she'd been in high school, if not sexier, in that short red dress that clung to every curve. We danced, till the party ended. Then we found a dark corner at a bar and sipped drinks until closing. She told me about her husband and his business, how they'd met. I went on about my army days and my private detective agency, doing my best to make mundane work sound exciting. I confided about my ruined marriage with Cheryl.

Hannah held my hand beneath the table. She looked down at her drink. Tears welled in her eyes. "You may be the lucky one, Stan. At least you knew enough to end yours." I kissed her hand. She changed the subject, telling me about her son heading off to college. I said, "I remember when *we* left for college … separately."

"My big mistake," she said. In the end we ordered an Uber and a taxi, headed in different directions.

Maybe it was just my male ego, but she'd been attracted to me that night. I hadn't stopped fantasizing about her since. Her call flashing on my dashboard, lit up more than just the screen.

"IF SHE MESSED YOU UP, I bet she had reason," I said. I waited, but Bud went quiet. The phone rang again, and I answered. Hannah's voice came out of the dashboard speakers. "Hey, Stan."

"I'm here with Bud Randolph," I said.

"Oh, … hello, Bud."

"Some coincidence that your friend Bud is with me," I said.

"Did he tell you what happened between us?"

"Nope."

"Bud used to work for me in a job he hated."

I shifted, leaning back against the car door, so I could look straight at him.

Bud opened his door. "You pretended you were helping me, but you didn't do me any favors." He said this to the dashboard, before jumping out and stalking away.

"He's gone," I said. "Now you can tell me why you called."

She waited a few seconds and said, "I need you." I felt warm blood rising inside my chest. "It's my husband, Jake. He's gone missing." Her voice went soft. "I hope you'll help me, Stan."

I wondered if *helping her* was a great idea, with her married and me leaping to a romantic fantasy before reeling myself in. Outside, I saw Bud stomping back toward me. He plopped into the back seat and closed the door.

"He's back," I announced.

I heard Hannah take in a breath on the phone.

"Hello Bud, Look, I'm sorry for how things went."

"Sure."

"You didn't give me a choice," Hannah said.

Bud glowered. "I know that."

"I had a job to do, and you—"

"You're going to say I pissed everyone off."

"The customers, Bud. You lost us business."

"I get it; you expected me to shut up and drive them where they wanted to go."

I thought of trying to make peace, but Bud held up his hand. "And okay, goddamn it, you were right. There, now I said it. Can we move on?"

"I actually liked you," she said. "A little, anyway. You were funny, but you didn't belong working there."

"Which of your careers was that?" I asked.

"Driving a limo for rich pricks, too dainty to drive themselves to work."

"You informed them of that opinion?"

Bud grinned. "That was the fun part of the job."

"She needs our help," I said. He didn't jump at me, so I asked her, "Are you at home?"

"Yes."

I kept my eyes on Bud, with his ironic smirk, as she gave me the address. "We'll be there in twenty."

"Thanks." She hung up.

I said, "I like this woman, okay? She's not a suspect. She's not your boss. Her marriage is on the rocks, and now her husband's gone missing."

"Poor baby." Bud reached forward from the backseat and patted my shoulder. "That gleam in your eyes, partner—you got the hots for this babe?"

"There was something between us once," I conceded. "I saw her one night last year and it felt good."

CHAPTER 6

BUD

I sat in the back, as Stan drove to Hannah's place, keeping any Covid germs to myself.

We rolled into Hannah's upscale, snooty neighborhood, all phony Tudor facades, beams and stucco—perfect place for a tricky bitch's lair. She opened the door wearing a mask, blue surgical, like the one Stan had on. She touched Stan's arm and blinked her fake lashes at him, her eye shadow sexy blue. Her hair was auburn down by her shoulders, but a couple of inches ran black from the part. Another pandemic freak-case.

She wore a pale green, fleece jogging suit that showed off her amazing derriere, as she led us down the hall. Stan followed her pretty close, keeping me back and blocking the view. The two of them planted their butts at opposite corners of the white leather sofa. They un-masked, never taking their eyes off each other.

I began exploring the living room, doing my best to distract Hannah from my partner. Pretentious friggin' house with floor to ceiling glass, looking out to a swimming pool, small green lawn, and pine trees. The coffee table was a glass plate resting on a mermaid statue, topless. –Nice. I checked out the golden trophies in a case; swimming and archery, tennis; and a few expensive-looking paintings on the wall. Whatever her husband did for a living, he was raking it in.

Hannah glanced my way once in a while, but then went right back to wooing Stan with those hot hazel eyes. Brazen bitch.

I plopped down close to her on the couch. Hannah's whole body jerked. She leapt up and landed in a leather armchair. Mission accomplished.

"Nice place." I ogled the bare-breasted mermaid under the coffee table and smirked at Hannah.

Stan glared at me. —He could be that way—and asked Hannah, "You said your husband … Jake? He's been gone how long?"

"A month. He goes on these business trips."

"But you've heard from him?"

The shrew blushed. "Only once."

I snorted for fun. "Great marriage." I figured Stan was giving me the hard looks, but I kept watching Hannah.

"He and I had been on the outs but testing the idea of getting back together." She sighed. "Jake's been upset lately, a little flaky. I don't think he would do anything, wouldn't hurt himself." Her voice broke.

I thought she'd bury her face in her hands, like some over-the-top soap opera heroine, but she held that for the second act.

"One of the strange things; he started quoting the bible. He did that sometimes early in our marriage, but he hadn't in a long time. I figured he was trying to come to grips with something, so I gave him space." She looked close to tears. Manipulative. She pulled a paper out of the pouch in her sweat shirt and leaned over the coffee table passing it across to Stan. "This is all I have from him."

Stan read it and tossed it to me. Dated a month back:

Hannah, dear, this is my poor attempt at apology. I'm sorry I missed our dinner the other night. I had to fly to India on short notice for business. In the rush to pack and get to the airport, our date slipped my mind. I can't believe I did that!

This trip will take some time. I have to go on to Indonesia. Now for the hard part. Is there a right way to tell you this? You've said you want to patch things up. I do too, but I'm getting used to living apart. It feels almost comfortable now.

I have stuff to think about. Our relationship, of course. Lots of junk from my past too. When a man's alone, he has time to mull over old wounds and mistakes. Mine have been boiling inside me, coming to the surface. I hope you'll understand if I don't get in touch right away.

I do love you.

Jake

"He just cut out on you, Hannah?" Stan asked.

"I can't believe he treated me that way. He hasn't contacted me or Luke since. –Luke's our son."

Great opening. "Was your husband his father?" I asked. "Or—"

"Stop it, Bud," Stan snapped.

"All right, I'll be constructive. This email is bullshit."

Stan ignored that and asked her, "Have you called the police?"

"A detective came yesterday, older guy, over fifty. I showed him the email. 'You're good looking,' he said. 'But your hubby needed a break.' The cop was kind enough to add, 'Lots of good-looking gals in In-do-nes-ia.'" Hannah pressed her knuckles against her cheek, then dropped the hand back into her lap. "I wanted to scream. Before he walked out the door, the son of a bitch said, 'You have a really fine day now.'"

"I don't get it," Stan said. "Jake flew off with the virus rampant all over the world. I didn't think they'd let you do that."

Hannah stood up, looking nervous and confused, really hamming it up. She stretched, giving Stan a good look at her profile. "Jake's a guy who ignores rules. He always finds a way." She headed toward the bar.

"Good for him. It's all fake," I said. "Corona virus boloney."

"It's not," Stan said. "He's been reckless."

She set a couple of glasses on the bar. "I'm worried. I want you to find him."

Stan gaped at her. "We're not cops. We're barely investigators. I mean …"

Hannah, the cold bitch who'd fired me without a *sorry* or a few dollars in severance, had Stan helpless in the palms of her cleavage. If he, naïve *schmuck*, became involved with this married bitch, what would that do to our friendship? I waited a beat and said, "Personally, I think we should walk out of here and forget you asked. But Stan, Stan's the kinda guy who can't say no."

Hannah ignored me and gave Stan an adoring smile. "You can do this, Stan. You told me after the reunion. You have the background."

Who knew what Stan had said to impress her? He and I had run some inquiries back in our Army days, mostly about soldiers who'd gotten drunk and pissed off the locals. Then Stan had worked five years in SimiBank's fraud department. He left that job to open our agency, where difficult cases were rare as three eyed snakes.

Hannah poured a glass of white wine. "You're Scotch and water, right, Stan?"

"Water at a minimum." Stan leaned toward me and murmured, "Take it easy. Her husband's missing."

He got up and walked to the bar. The way their eyes were making out with each other made me want to puke. And her being separated from her husband might give Stan an excuse.

"So, you and my partner used to screw around?"

"Shut up," Stan said.

"You dumped Stan back then. Now you're begging for his help?"

She gave Stan a girly, he's-wounded-me look.

"I didn't tell him that." Stan said it low, but I heard.

I grinned really wide. "Thanks for asking. I'd love a gin and tonic."

"Bar's closed," she said.

Stan moved close to her, raising his hand, like he was about to touch her hair. He lowered it and took the drink from the bar. "I could stay a while," he said.

"Sounds really good, Stan."

"Hello," I said. "I'm here in the room with you."

She was his old, hot girlfriend. I was just his homely pal. I didn't have a chance, but I had to try. "Hey, Stan, let's get out of here. Take your drink to go."

Stan took the Escape's key fob out of his pocket and tossed it over. "You go, Bud. I'll stay and get the information about Hannah's husband."

Nothing for me to do but propel my ass out of there.

CHAPTER 7

STAN

Bud left, and Hannah led me to the sofa. We embraced, both masked and trying not to breathe on each other. She told me how lonely she'd felt, how sweet it was to be with me, how handsome and smart I was. We didn't say much after that, just savored the closeness.

"I've always cared about you, Stan." She said that, just as I stepped out her front door to catch my Uber home.

Back in my bed I felt drowsy from the scotch, but imaginings kept me awake. My heart felt the thrill of her … and the pain. She'd been a girl back when she'd hurt me, off to college, exposed to a world of lecherous boys. Now she was a mature woman. If she said I was a comfort to her, she meant it. If her eyes adored me, they meant it.

Besides her affection, Hannah's case sparked my interest. In my old job at SimiBank, I'd followed leads and solved cases. I'd felt capable. That feeling evaporated, as my marriage blew up and my job went down the tubes. I'd settled for the easy money of workers' comp cases. If I could help Hannah, she'd respect me. She'd regret betraying me back then. Maybe I'd appreciate myself a little more. All I had to do was find Jake Christian.

THE NEXT MORNING, I drove while Bud questioned me from the Escape's back seat.

"Where we goin', Stanley?"

"Hannah's husband has a partner."

"So you're going to help that pretty bitch."

"Don't call her that. The partner claims Jake sent him emails." —Interesting, now I was on a first name basis with Hannah's missing husband.

Bud leaned forward over the seat, and I cranked my window the rest of the way down.

"Objective observation number one," he said. "Mrs. Hannah Christian is not all shaken up over her missing husband—missing for weeks, not hours."

Bud hadn't seen her the way I had last night. She hadn't sobbed quietly in *his* arms.

"She is, or she wouldn't have swallowed her pride to call me."

Bud snickered. "Objective observation number two: When you weren't looking, she sent me a few sexy glances, even though she hates my ass." He paused for a moment and added, "When this is done, she'll toss you like a scummy rubber."

I took a swipe at him with the back of my hand. He blocked it and flopped back in his seat. I wanted to laugh and to fire him, both at the same time.

"Observation three: I see why you're taken with her. She's beautiful in a sneaky way."

Bud couldn't see Hannah's beauty as I did, his head all full of conspiracy nonsense and negativity. Those soft hazel eyes; that shy, soulful smile. Her look conveyed sympathy, warmth, caring, and now deep worry.

"The husband's done with her—the way you should be, Stan. I'm just sayin' as your friend. You can't see it, 'cause you've got a fuckin' thing for her."

He was wrong. I'd barely seen her since I was eighteen.

"Hannah says Jake always called every few days, even when they were on the outs. They're trying to get together again. He wouldn't just—"

"He wants the hell out and doesn't have the balls to tell her."

"He hasn't been in touch with the son either."

"Yeah," Bud conceded. "I'll give you that."

"It'll be good for us working like real detectives." I said it, not sure we had a chance of finding Jake Christian. "And we'll make some extra dough. Money to pay for your root canal." I'd footed the bill for that, and Bud owed me.

"You get an advance from her?" he asked.

I hadn't actually mentioned money with Hannah. "The partner's name is Sirjay. Hannah doesn't trust him."

"Sergei?"

"No, not one of our president's Russian friends." I couldn't resist the dig, but didn't want Bud to start in on one of his Trump-athons. "Jacob Christian's partner, Sirjay Malik."

"Hindu?"

I looked in the mirror and saw Bud grinning.

"Be nice, even if he speaks with an accent."

Bud, still amused— "Like our president, I am the least prejudiced guy you'll ever meet."

Right.

WE ARRIVED AT A PARKING LOT dominated by a wide storefront, big glass windows like a furniture store, huge sign: *Sir Jacob Antiquities, Purveyors of Priceless Artifacts.*

"Hang back for a minute," Bud said.

I drove to a corner of the parking lot and pulled into a space near a liquor store. *What now?*

"If something happened to Christian, his partner's involved. We need leverage."

"We have only our good looks and your wacky theories."

"Wrong," Bud reached over from the backseat and handed me an I.D. wallet. "I knew we'd need these someday."

I flipped it open and saw a gold star on one side, an ID card with the inscription, *Los Angeles County Investigator*, on the other.

"What the heck, Bud? We could get screwed for this."

Still, we were doing it for Hannah. Maybe he was right about leverage.

"Go ahead," Bud said. "Park in front of the store. We'll walk in like a couple of confident hombres."

I did what he demanded, because, because, because at heart I'm a fool. Bud jumped out before I'd stopped the car. I ditched the badge under the driver's seat and followed him in. The showroom was jammed with tables full of silver icons; free-standing pottery elephants; a six-foot blue Hindu man-god; a fierce, glowering totem dude.

A man came toward us; dark skin, middle height, 60-ish. He eyed Bud's badge, giving a little twitch of the lips but no wide-eyed surprise. "Sirjay Malik, at your service."

He had a plump face with soft brown eyes, dark curly hair, and an accent a little like the owner of the great curry place over on Fifth.

"You the owner?" I asked.

"Half-owner. I have a partner."

"Jacob Christian," Bud said. "He hasn't been around for a while."

Malik harrumphed. "With Jake a week on a business trip turns to a month."

"Mad at him?" Bud asked.

"He does our advertising. It has gone stale without him, and his travel expenses …" He raised his hands as if imploring Vishnu for relief. "What can I do for you?"

"On your website," I said. "It says the largest collection of genuine antique Buddhas outside Tibet."

Malik shook his head. "Jake's idea. He exaggerates. We used to sell strictly from India, but my partner insisted we add Indonesia. His business trips cost a fortune."

"Sacred stones that cure gout?" I said. "Another exaggeration?"

"We have no such things." Malik avoided my eyes. "Embellishment. It's part of advertising. It's all—"

Bud blurted, "Your partner is full of shit."

Malik stood shaking his head.

"This crap embarrasses you," Bud said. "It's written all over your face."

I watched, feeling somewhere between appalled and intrigued at Bud's attack-dog style.

Malik sighed. "Yes. Yes. OK. Jake's not scrupulous about details, but—"

"Jacob Christian's wife says he's missing," I said.

"*Estranged* wife," Malik said. "She called me, and I explained to her—"

"She thinks you're a creep," Bud added.

No. No. No. If this guy was dangerous, I didn't want Hannah in his sights. "She didn't say that."

Malik looked hurt for an instant, and then Bud said, "Look. You know and we know, your partner's dead. Tell us where to find the body, and we'll help you."

Yikes.

Malik's eyes went wide, mine too, and he shook his head.

"Self-defense, right?" Bud gave Malik a look; friendly, conspiratorial; something he'd seen on TV. "We can work with that."

Malik flinched at the sound of the bell by the front door. A brunette entered leading a toddler by the hand.

Malik hissed, "He's not dead. I'll tell you. Come. Come."

He hustled us off to an office in back.

I halted in the doorway. "Not yours. Show us Jake Christian's space."

Malik glanced back toward the showroom. He sighed and led us to the other office.

CHAPTER 8

BUD

When Malik left, Stan hustled to the file cabinet. I headed for the big mahogany desk. I slid the top drawer open. Only a couple of blank legal pads and a few pens in there, a carton of breath mints in the drawer below. Disappointing.

I looked over at Stan, who was thumbing through the cabinet. "Do you think I'm being too hard on this jerk, partner?"

"Hannah said Malik is slippery. Go ahead; play super cop." Stan went back to work, but then he looked up again. "No fake badges after today. You hear me?"

I liked the first part of what he said. The bit about badges; that was just Stan being Stan. I moved on to the bottom drawer, finding only some invoice forms and a toiletries bag with a razor and shave cream, toothpaste and brush, a comb. I heard a sound and looked up.

Malik stood in the doorway, clearing his throat and glowering. I dumped the stuff into the drawer with a clatter and straightened up. Malik went for the window, and I hustled after him. Malik opened it. When he turned, I was in his face. Malik gave silly shooing gestures with both hands, which I ignored. He whipped a black mask from a back pocket, slipped it on and gave me a look, more scared than pissed. Super.

"What you said, sir is offensive. My partner is not dead, and, and, and I am a peaceful man, sir. I certainly don't kill people."

"Sit." I pointed at the desk chair. Malik slithered past me and sat, looking resentful and pretty fucking guilty. I was on to something! Behind the guy, pottery Buddhas and other junk jammed the shelves. Total shit shop.

"Jake Christian is a strange fellow," Malik said.

"A liar," I pointed out. "An embarrassment." This was sure fun.

Malik straightened in his chair. "Yes, but that doesn't mean ..." He looked from me to Stan, a sick, sad grin on his lips. "Here's the truth: My partner's lies are the least of it. Maybe his *estranged* wife didn't tell you this, but she knows." Malik ran one hand across the palm of the other, then held them out to me. "When we first met, he had red welts on his hands; ugly, like raw meat, right in the middle."

"Both hands?" I pictured chunks of rib-eye in Malik's palms.

Malik nodded. "He wore gloves much of the time, but I saw. Later, he had plastic surgery to cover them. He's a jittery fellow too, hatching schemes all hours of the night. And, and he acquired *that dog.*" Malik pointed to a four-foot tall, lacquered collie statue in the corner of the office. I'd seen it when we walked in, but hadn't thought about it. "He paid two thousand for it, company money, but it sits in this office like his personal puppet. Once, Jake interrupted our discussion about advertising to ask that *creature* for its opinion." Malik shook his head. "And this too; I came upon him last month in the store, holding a Hindu statue in his hand, the elephant god, Ganesha. I stopped to listen. Jake was telling the idol about Jesus and his magical healing power. If he leaves for a month instead of a week, it's not your worry. It's a relief for me, if you must know."

Pretty fucking weird.

Stan picked up a picture from the cadenza and held it out— Jake in a tux with Hannah, looking slinky in a lavender evening gown. "How was your personal relationship with them?"

Good idea, Stan.

Malik pulled out a handkerchief and wiped sweat from his forehead. "We were not close." He corrected— "We *are* not close. With my Indian contacts and Jake's talent for sales, we do all right." Malik gave Stan a pleading look, itching to be done with us. "Look. I have customers."

"Yeah, sure. That little girl in the showroom is going to want a fake antique elephant." I moved in, leaning on the desk. "You claim to be peaceful. You're some kinda Hindu, right?"

Malik tilted as far away as he could, while still seated. "I am no longer of that faith, but that's none of your concern."

Stan came over and laid a hand on my elbow. *Good cop routine; yeah, that might work.* Stan shook his head. "Mister Malik, you and I understand about difficult partners. I see that you were friendly with the deceased."

Fantastic. Stan was catching on.

Malik opened his mouth, closed it again, swallowed and said, "*Not deceased.* He's on business." He grinned suddenly and shook a finger at Stan. "Wait. Better. Better. Better. *Better.* He sent emails, one quite recent. If you hadn't attacked me so, I would have thought of this earlier." He shot me a nasty squint. "Please step back." He looked cautiously at Stan. "Can you make him move out of the way?"

I stepped aside.

Malik moved past and led us to his office. He sat behind a stainless steel, kidney-shaped desk and typed on his computer. His printer spit out two sheets of paper. He waved them at us. "You'll see. Jake was purchasing Hindi dolls in Mumbai. Now he's bound for Indonesia for teak statues and whatnot."

Stan took the pages without looking at them. The Indian guy looked smug now, but I wasn't done with him.

Not Hindu, huh? Tell you the truth: I can't get enough of all those crazy-as-crap religions—churches where they dance holding rattlesnakes, Jim Jones and his Kool-Aid drinkers, even your run of the mill Hare Krishnas chanting Ommmmmmm to some Hindu god-head.

"If you ain't Hindu, what then?"

"Confucian, sir. I believe in good acts."

"Hannah Christian is quite a babe," I said. "Even a Buddhist can appreciate—"

"*Confucian*, not Buddhist *or* Hindu." Sirjay Malik gave a smarmy half-smile. "We had a few dinners is all, *the three of us*, together."

"Sure. Your fling with his wife; you want to deny that too."

"Enough." Malik, grim-faced, stood and pointed to the door. "Please, sirs, depart now."

Stan nodded to me. "Go on, Bud. I'll be out in a minute."

I walked outside and settled in the back seat of the Escape. Stan showed up a few minutes later, looking pleased with himself. He got in and handed me a sheet of paper. "Jacob Christian's resumé."

"You wouldn't have gotten that if I didn't flash my badge," I said.

Stan eyed me in the mirror. "So, what do you think about Jake Christian now?"

"No computer in Christian's office. He'd have taken a laptop on his business trip."

"You don't think he's dead?"

"Nah. He's in friggin' Bali."

Stan gaped. "You were all over Malik about killing his partner."

"You know me." I did a little drum roll, thumping the seat back. "All the world's a stage, and I'm a humble actor pretending to be a detective."

"Still, a month's a heck of a long time not to communicate with his gorgeous wife and his son." Stan started the car and backed up.

"What's that crap about Christian preaching Jesus to a statue? And scars on his hands?" *Pretty fucking intriguing.* "*Stigmata?* Are you getting it, Stan? You know what I'm talking about?"

"Yeah, the marks Jesus had after the crucifixion."

"Weird, ain't it?"

"Malik might have told us more, but he's pretty unhappy thanks to your holy inquisition."

"You think I went too far?"

Stan laughed. "I should have fired you months ago."

"You know," I offered. "You gotta up your game, Stan. If you want to be a real detective, get in the suspect's face. Call him a *shit-head* a few times. That gets 'em talking."

Stan just shook his head, grinning.

"Stigmata, man, Yowzers." I settled back in my seat to let my little gray cells ponder that idea.

CHAPTER 9

JEFF

1988, OKLAHOMA

After Jeff's encounter with the cultivator, his mother bandaged his palm and slathered makeup on the back of his hand. At school he tried to keep his right hand out of sight, his fingers closed over the bandage.

One evening a few weeks later, his momma came home, her eyes lit with joy. "While you were at school, I went to a meeting all the way over in Tulsa, Jeff. There was a minister there, so much more holy than our Reverend Garner. God flew all around me. I felt Him. God touched all of us in that room."

She frowned and plopped into an armchair. "I feel a little sick, Jeff. Touch me and make me better." He touched her hand and she said, "Now with your right hand. Press it to my cheek."

Years later, he remembered the way she'd seemed so tall standing over him that day in the garden. He recalled her fascination with the blood and the way she seemed really happy right then. Five-year-old Jeff was confused by his mother's behavior. It was years before he learned the word *bizarre*.

TWO YEARS LATER, 1990-91

JEFF COULDN'T REMEMBER much about his dad, not even his voice, but he sure missed him. When other kids boasted about their fathers, Jeff walked away. What he remembered best were those times at their cabin in the New Mexico desert. Jeff and his mother hadn't returned there since his dad passed, three years back, but he still felt the peacefulness of that place on the mesa and the steady hand of his father guiding them. (Even his mother had seemed cheerful.)

Now that he was seven, Jeff attended bible class five times a week and adult services on Sunday. His mother began reading scripture from the podium before Reverend Garner delivered his sermons. Jeff didn't know why, but his mom's talks seemed to annoy the reverend. Many of their fellow parishioners, Reverend Garner's friends, avoided Jeff's mother, which also made no sense. She was such a good and holy woman. At school, he had to throw balls with his left hand because of his injury. The boys laughed and shouted. "Jeffy, you throw like a girl."

"Those filthy boys don't matter," his momma said. "Not one bit, because you're special."

His arithmetic wasn't good and his reading just average, so he didn't understand how he could be special. Still, Momma said that over and over, so it had to be true. To make him more special, she had Jeff read aloud from the good book, read loud and clear to her, practicing for *his future*.

JEFF TURNED EIGHT. His mom greeted him after school one day, laughing, hugging him, beaming a radiant smile. "A revival is coming, son."

"What?"

"A holy gathering. God's special preacher, Simon Love, will join us to share the Word. They'll set up a tent out at the fairgrounds, so hundreds of people can hear. You know what else?"

Jeff shook his head.

"He's famous, and he's coming because I wrote to him. There's sin in our town, and I told him how badly we need his righteous vision."

Jeff knew about the Word and about vision from his mom's speeches at church, which were starting to exceed the pastor's homilies. Reverend Garner had asked her to stop, but every Sunday, she marched to the podium and every Sunday, the reverend stood helpless.

"I'm going to be up on that big stage with Reverend Love, Jeff. You'll get to meet him." She laughed. "I'll tell him what an exceptional boy you are. You know the mark you have; it came from God." She hadn't mentioned that before, but, as he thought about it that night, about Jesus and His crucifixion and about his own hand, still raw and red from all the times he couldn't resist poking, it made sense.

For the next week, Jeff's mom fed him the meals he enjoyed most, telling him how proud he made her and how Reverend Love was going to enjoy meeting him. She squeezed his hand, and he winced. She dug her fingernail into the sore in his palm, until a drop of blood appeared. Was it really something special, as Momma said, or just the place where her cultivator pierced him?

"I have a plan, Jeff, an exceptional plan. It will be summer soon. You'll be off school. You and I ..." He tensed, thinking she might jab his hand again but she didn't. "You and I will travel with Pastor Love and preach with him."

Jeff had gone up to the pulpit with his mother a few times in their little church. He'd read short passages of the bible to the people. But this sounded scary. Strangers would gawk at them.

That Saturday night, a stage and hundreds of chairs filled a big tent outside town. Reverend Love, a tall, white-haired man in his sixties, smiled down at three hundred people. He wore a long black gown that made him seem to glide across the stage. The congregants all wore their Sunday best. A few that Jeff didn't recognize, with wheelchairs or crutches, sat at the front, just below the stage. Jeff's mother occupied a chair onstage, looking blissful, honored for having invited the reverend to town. At the opposite side of the stage, a young blond woman in a short white dress, blew kisses to the crowd.

The preacher towered over the microphone. "Brothers and sisters, we gather under the gaze of our Lord, in the light of our Lord, under His skies and His heaven." He gestured to the sky and then looked toward Jeff's mother. She rose from her chair, but the reverend turned back to the crowd. "I have come because your city lives in sin. I have but two days to heal you, heal you all."

Jeff's mother blushed and sank back down. The reverend preached hell fire and brimstone for the next hour and a half. He commanded those with crutches to walk free, and they did. He touched a man in a wheelchair on the head. The man rose and shouted, 'Alleluia.' Reverend Love praised Jesus, God, for healing the infirm, with a booming voice that cascaded to the heights of the tent and reverberated in the chests of the men, women and children. He cursed all men as sinners, and he never again looked at Jeff's mom.

Jeff felt her disappointment, as they walked to the reverend's hotel. They found his suite and entered. While they waited for a dozen well-wishers to depart, Jeff couldn't take his eyes off the white marble fireplace, the beautiful paintings, and the gold framed mirrors on the walls in the reverend's suite.

Finally, the others left. The reverend sat, relaxed in a red velvet arm chair that matched the carpeting in the room. A polished wooden table sat beside him with a glass of amber liquid, maybe iced tea, Jeff thought. His blond assistant stood by.

Reverend Love extended a welcoming hand to them.

Jeff's mother held back, wringing her hands. "Reverend Love." The name came out shaky. She stopped to clear her throat. "I'm glad you came to our town."

"You were right to send for me," he said. "Your neighbors are sinners. You, dear lady, are doing the Lord's bidding."

His mom straightened and moved in closer. "I have something to offer. I've been speaking out at church."

The reverend snorted and gestured to the blonde who produced a bottle of whiskey from a cabinet and poured for him. Whiskey!

"If you'd let me say a few words tomorrow night at the meeting … I could introduce you," his mother said.

When the reverend agreed, she thanked him and led Jeff away.

"Momma, you were going to tell the reverend how special I am."

"Tomorrow."

"Momma, he was drinking liquor! You called that 'the devil's drink.'"

"Don't you worry about that, Jeff. The reverend is going to help with our mission."

THE NEXT DAY Jeff's mother locked herself in her bedroom, "to get prepared," she said. That night, four hundred people crowded the tent. Jeff's momma looked as beautiful as he'd ever seen her, her long dress a dazzling white in the spotlights. She strode to the microphone on its silver stand, and took a deep breath. "I'm Sarah Little," she announced. "Many of you know me." She seemed to search the crowd for someone, for Jeff? No, she didn't look at him. She spoke toward somebody near the back row on his left. "I love you," she called. "God loves you most of all." She searched again, focusing on someone to his right now. "God will heal you, if you give Him the chance." She pointed toward another part of the crowd. "And you. And you."

Jeff had never seen his mother like this—so confident and strong—not even when she read scripture at their little church. He saw Reverend Love watching from the side of the stage, his jaw tight.

"The holy book tells us that we will all be judged," she shouted. "We must meet our Maker. We must love the Lord, if we are to be saved."

His mother shifted her gaze again and stretched her hand toward congregants behind Jeff. "Take my hand and I will lead you to the promised land." She looked back at Reverend Love. "Take Reverend Love's hand. Follow him, for he will save you."

The reverend stepped forward and came shoulder to shoulder with her. Jeff wasn't sure, but he might have nudged her a little. His mother retreated to her seat, wearing a radiant smile.

Afterward, they met the reverend in his hotel room. The preacher sat back in his arm chair, the glass of amber liquid on its table beside him, his young assistant waiting off to the side.

Jeff stayed a couple of steps back, as his momma approached the man. "What did you think?"

"Pardon me?"

"When I spoke, what did you think of it?"

Reverend Love smirked. "Oh, you want me to thank you."

"I want to take up the challenge," she said.

The minister picked up the glass, examined the liquid and set it down. "What do you mean, dear lady?"

"God's challenge. I want to join you and preach the Word."

The man's eyes widened. He chuckled, as he ran his eyes over her. "You are an attractive woman. You had a fine moment tonight. I trust you savored it, but, madam, I'm a one man show. I speak. I have this pretty *young* woman to assist." He waved at his assistant. "Younger, blonder, and even prettier than you, I might say."

Jeff's mom stared at the evangelist. "God means for me to do this, and I can prove it."

Reverend Love clucked his tongue. "Dear, dear Mrs. Little, I did you a courtesy tonight. I appreciate what you said about me, but that is—"

"Please, let me show you." She took Jeff by the wrist and pulled him forward. She ripped the bandage from his palm. Jeff winced, and tears filled his eyes.

Reverend Love stared at the raw wound. He banged his glass down on the table and jumped to his feet. "*Stop.* Do not embarrass yourself or this boy further."

His mother retreated a step, releasing Jeff's hand. He wanted to run, but he stood frozen. She stared at the reverend in disbelief. "Can't you—"

"Mrs. Little, I am God's messenger. The boy is just a boy. Do you understand?" Reverend Love hulked over her. Jeff's mother shrunk like a dog about to be whipped.

She glanced at Jeff's face and then at his hand. "But, but ..."

"You praise the Lord, and you do not question. You are a *woman*, and I am *He*. Is that clear?"

His mom slunk to the polished wooden door, turned its sculpted brass knob and rushed out, with Jeff right behind.

They hurried along Main Street, heading into the residential area. He wanted to comfort her, but didn't know how. "What happened? You were going to preach with Reverend Love. I was coming with you."

"Hush, boy." She walked still faster.

"Momma, when you showed him my hand, you said he'd see."

She turned on him, grabbed his wrist and yanked. "You are not good enough."

"But."

She slapped him. He covered his face and began sobbing.

She glared at him. "I looked at that man who holds the spirit of God Almighty in his hands. I looked at your hand and your hang-dog face, and I saw what the reverend saw."

Jeff could hardly breathe.

"You are not special enough, little boy." She smiled in a shocking, mean way and then brightened. "Someday you will be."

The next day, Jeff watched, as his mom paced the living room, from worn-out sofa to broken-down fireplace. "The school you go to is godless. They can't understand you there. I'll teach you from now on." She stopped and took Jeff's shoulders in her hands. "You and I *will* fulfill God's challenge. We *will* sacrifice all to Him." She let him go and crossed the room again. "Another thing, son; from now on, I'll be known as Sarah *Lamb*. You will be Jeff Lamb." The gentle way she touched him eased Jeff's fears. She truly did love him.

CHAPTER 10

STAN

The next morning Bud insisted on picking me up at 6:40 with the cryptic words, "I gotta show you something." For once Bud drove, in his Mustang, with me in back.

"What, you got, Bud?"

"Cracked another case, partner."

I let myself enjoy his self-satisfied grin for a moment. "Great, Bud. By the way, we have to split up for the afternoon."

He gave me a curious look by way of the rearview mirror.

"I'm heading to the fairgrounds for a Covid test."

"Covid eh? You got symptoms?" Bud scrutinized me in the mirror, actually looking a little worried. "Or you think it's hot to have some babe ram a Q-tip up your *schnoz*?"

I felt myself blush and looked ahead at the road. "Hannah asked me to get one. I called her last night to tell her about Malik and she …" I realized I was smirking like a fool. "What do you think that means?"

"She might put out for you, Stan. Who knows, but when you find her hubby, she'll stomp you like a stinkbug."

"She's starting to care about me again."

"You're thinking with your gonads, my friend. That's really dumb, when it comes to Hannah bitch-face Christian."

"Heck, Bud I shouldn't have told you about this. It's between the two of us."

Bud seemed to think that over for a second and said, "You have an itch of doubt about Hannah, don't you, Stan. You need my practical insights, and you know it. So, what else did she say?"

It was stupid, confiding in Bud, but he was, despite all common sense, my closest friend.

"She said she's been worried, and it felt really good having me there the other night." I could still hear her voice, sweet and seductive. "I'm steady, and she needs that right now."

"Jesus, Stan. You're buying that?"

I let Bud's comments sink in, as he drove me to a suburban neighborhood and parked in front of a grey and white craftsman style house. He made a big deal of eyeing his watch. "Let's go. It's after seven."

Bud led the way to the side of the house. "Wait till I show you what this phony shit-head is up to," Bud opened the gate beside the house. "It's okay, we got permission."

A couple of wooden crates sat by the back fence. Bud whispered, "Our suspect lives back there." He climbed onto one of the boxes and motioned for me to join him. I moved my box a few feet from him and stepped up.

There was a brown house ninety feet away with a green canvas canopy suspended over a set of professional-looking gym equipment. I hunkered down low over the fence, but it probably didn't matter. Our subject, a thick-set guy in a cut off sweatshirt, faced away from us, doing deep squats. He spent a couple of minutes stretching his hamstrings, then jumped onto a rowing machine, going at it hard. The machine grated away, as the ropes ripped through their pulleys.

Bud murmured, "I made friends with this guy." He gestured at the grey and white house behind us. "Every day he hears this noise right about seven-fifteen."

"You videoed this?"

Bud grinned. "You bet."

"This is Busby, right? The fireman?"

"Jones, truck driver."

"You have the evidence, so why'd you get me up this early?"

"We're going to bust his ass bigtime for workers comp fraud. I get the credit, right boss?"

Funny the way Bud, who acted so aloof, craved my approval. "Yeah, *partner*. You did good." Whenever I called him that, I knew it made his day, and making Bud happy felt pretty good.

CHAPTER 11

THE BODY

October 2020, The mine pit near Navajo country

Movement. A hand, an eyelid flitting. Eyes opened. Muscles ached, arm throbbed—broken? The person, lying on a tarp at the bottom of the shaft, rolled over, looked up, and saw a patch of sky overhead, stars. There was enough moon glow to make out a pebbly dirt floor, bottles, cans of some sort … a book.

The morning sky was clear, praise the Lord. The cans became provisions—Spam, beans, corn, tuna. The book became a bible, Old Testament; that made sense. All these things were strewn across another tarp nearby. There was a can opener, blankets, toilet paper, a small propane heater, a half dozen large bags of Cheetos. All the comforts of home.

CHAPTER 12

STAN

A person might think I'm nuts to employ a guy like Bud.

As I mentioned, Bud's real name is Andy, a great name, which he rejects. Bud/Andy and I served in an Army MP unit in Iraq, investigating our fellow soldiers. In our spare time we bonded over beers, speculating about the futility of the war. We'd both believed in the mission until no weapons of mass destruction turned up. Then Bud went skeptical. —He plays that role to perfection. I kept on believing. We'd diminished Saddam Hussein to a bearded hermit, hiding down a well.

Nine months in the war. Bud and I rode with some other soldiers in a Humvee headed to Fallujah one day. We were lucky; we got out that time. The guys who continued on weren't as fortunate. We were blown up a month later. Not as bad as those guys, not fatal, but with concussions and shrapnel wounds that sent us to Germany for treatment. In the hospital, our heads wrapped in gauze turbans, Bud showed me pictures of his sister, Cheryl. He told me about their childhood playmates and her boyfriends.

"My sis' doesn't have a steady guy now. She's a live one, Stan. Perfect for you."

Back in California, Bud introduced us—not much of a favor as it turned out. Cheryl's not just a *live one*; she's messed up. I spent lots of time during our marriage trying to arrange therapists and shrinks, bottles of pills, emergency room visits.

Cheryl decided I was cheating on her. I wasn't. Never did. I worked for SimiBank back then, investigating financial fraud. Cheryl's life took up far too much of my time. She'd call me for some emergency, often drug-induced, always imagined. Always I fell for it. My boss lectured me about setting an example for the other staff, employee discipline, morale. If she allowed me to spend so much "personal time" what would they all think? Yeah, what?

Another investigator at the bank drew a new case: Cheryl had taken out five (at least) fraudulent credit cards. They didn't fire me. I resigned after an argument with my boss—my fault, not hers.

Cheryl is just out of rehab now, according to Bud. Sorry, but I make a point of not contacting her directly. I can't save her. What I can do is help Bud. I promised Cheryl, and that's what I'll do as long as I can.

Things have been enjoyably calm since Cheryl went out of my life. The challenge of that job flew out the window at the same time. After all that chaos, a dull life seemed just fine.

Until now. Flirting with Hannah felt amazing. And that interview with Malik—the truth—when Bud made him squirm, it made my day.

The morning after my Covid test, I headed straight to our poor excuse for an office, in an industrial park, between a screen door installer and a shop that took the dings out of car doors—handy when a clumsy jerk parks next to you. The place has block walls painted pale yellow, two desks and an eight-foot faux-wood table. By opening the back window and front door, spreading out, wearing masks (when Bud cooperates), three of us can feel pretty safe. The third is our researcher, Melanie.

She was at her desk in the corner, with hot coffee ready in the pot. As usual, she wore her hair in a tight bun and draped herself in a loose shirt—this one khaki—and baggy pants, her white mask covered in blue daisies. With that mask and her purple thick-framed glasses, it could have been any black woman impersonating our computer whiz.

Mel worked for me part time and did free-lance jobs for SimiBank, the place I used to work. We'd been special friends back when we worked there; at least I'd thought so. When we went out for lunch with our co-workers, we *noticed* each other, with subtle glances. Once in a while, I'd stop by her office for a fifteen-minute chat. My marriage had been headed for the dumper. I didn't dump much of that on Mel, but she got the idea. She sympathized. She seemed happy most of the time and glad for my visits. Our talks lightened my day. I missed her when I left that job.

A couple of years later, running my company, S. Stein Investigations, I needed help with insurance inquiries. I decided that Mel could raise the computer IQ of my staff (Bud and me) and liven things up at the office. I invited her for burgers at an In-N-Out joint and joked with her about me being a big spender.

Mel surprised me that day. She chuckled at my joke, but not in the playful way I expected. Still, I tossed out the idea of a part time job.

She took a long, serious look at me and said, "Thanks, but are you sure that's a good idea?"

I took a moment to recover. Did she imagine we could be more than co-workers? Or she thought I did? Or some other reason it might be a mistake? I knew she'd be a great asset for S. Stein Investigations, whether or not she wanted to be friends.

"Strictly business," I assured her. We looked each other in the eye for a minute—no smiles.

"All right," she said. "I need a change, and I believe you. … Just so you know, I'm not looking for a relationship."

That comment stung, but it was better that way, right? — Just boss and employee. Later, thinking back on our lunch, I questioned my decision to hire her. The woman I'd hoped might liven things up, could serious them down instead.

Mel began working from home some days and spending three or four mornings a week at our office. She went on working afternoons for SimiBank.

She was almost my height, five-ten, and good looking. When she'd worked for the bank, she'd worn business suits that divulged little of her shape. Now, at my office, she continued to hide her looks with those glasses and loose clothing. I tried sometimes to get a better idea of the shape lurking beneath that blousy clothing. Something any guy would do, wasn't it?

Mel's personnel file contained only a few tax forms; Social Security number, address, phone. Only one dependent, herself. She had a couple of first-grade drawings stuck on the wall behind her computer. I was sure, almost, that she didn't have a child, but how would I know if she did?

After a couple of months, Mel lightened up a little, and then a bit more each week. She sent me a sweet brown-eyed smile, once in a while. She teased me in a low-key way. I mocked her back in my nerdy attempt at humor. Things were looking up.

I poured myself some coffee now. "Good morning, Mel. Hard at work, aye?"

She swiveled her chair toward me. "A gal like me, with two jobs, can't sleep in like her lazy-ass boss."

That made me smile. "I've told you, don't think of me so much as a boss, but …"

"I know, as a kind cousin who signs the checks." —One of the running jokes we'd begun recently. "That email you sent me about Jacob Christian," she said. "I haven't had a chance to look into it, with those new workers' comp cases to submit. I guess Bud caught that last guy lifting weights."

"He did, Mel. But let's put that off and track our missing Mr. Christian. His business partner's a guy named Malik, selling old stuff he calls *antiquities*. Jake was supposed to fly to India and Indonesia a month ago."

"Real detective work, Hey, Hey!"

"Right, Mel. If we track him down, it'll be like feathers in our caps." *Not to mention pleasing the lovely Hannah.*

"You got it, *boss*." She turned back to her computer.

Bud arrived. He and I spaced out by the table. We'd both read the email Malik had given us, dated two weeks before. I went over it now for the third time:

Greetings from Mumbai, Sirjay

> *I have some business to relate and also—I surprise myself—a few personal thoughts. We've not been close friends, I know, but you are an excellent partner, and I find that, sitting here in an Indian tea parlor, I have no one else to confide in. You may have guessed from the length of my absence; this trip has been far more than business—deeper and more exciting in every way, even bringing me closer to my spiritual past.*

Though we split up months ago, back home in the States, Hannah kept calling, wanting to get together and talk things out. I gave in to her due to my agreeable temperament, I guess. But now, halfway around the world, I'm freed of that burden. It would hurt her for me to say that, but now I don't have to say anything. She'll figure it out when I don't contact her. If she calls you, tell her I'm fine, but don't tell her this: Your people, the Hindus of India, are so accepting and warm. Not like the demanding females back home. I've found a lovely mistress here. And my son, Luke, as you know, we haven't had the best relationship. Ask Hannah to tell him I love him. That's even true.

Now to business. I've made some great acquisitions for the firm. You'll receive invoices by fax from Mumbai Industries. Once you pay them, you'll be amazed at the wealth of artifacts I've chosen. I'll be staying on for a while, so please wire another $50,000 to my personal account. That should cover business expenses (not to mention personal costs for me and my new lover). We can sort it out when I get home.

I'm chartering a boat to take my Hindu goddess on a romantic cruise across the Indian Ocean. No business on the cruise, but in Bali I'll get back to work. Sorry for the long email. I haven't ever said this, but I'm glad you're my partner.

Jacob

"Funny email, don't you think?" I asked. "All of a sudden, wanting to be buddies with the partner his wife hates."

"Hot wife that he wants to dump," Bud said.

"But a man far from home … loneliness can affect a person that way, and this pretty much clears our case," I offered.

Bud looked like he was about to unhook his mask. I aimed a finger at him, and he held up. "You think the guy's floating in the ocean, orgy-fying with this Indian babe?" Bud tossed his cell phone in the air and caught it. "Whoopie. I have a new theory."

"Of course."

Bud leaned forward across the table. "Let me run a couple of ideas by you—pretty fucking insightful, as you'll see. First, we've got *stigmata*, which is vital to the case."

"Yeah, right," I said.

"That stigmata factor is very damned cool. Second, Jacob Christian is dead, and his creepy Confucian partner did it."

"Ah, yuh. Yesterday it's alive, now dead … tomorrow? And you blame Sirjay Malik, why? Because he's Indian, right?"

"This is not *just* a conspiracy theory. Listen, my friend, because I'm right."

Melanie sat at her desk, staring at her PC, but listening. As usual, she shot me a glance once in a while, even as she worked. I knew because I kept glancing back.

When Bud shut up for a moment, she said, "Confucian? You don't find many of those walkin' 'round."

Bud tapped the table with his knuckles to get my attention. "You've heard of Ed Shin, right?"

"N-n-n-o."

"Come on, Stan. It's a famous case. I think this Hindu guy, Malik, pulled an *Ed Shin*. That's what I'm sayin'."

What tangent was Bud off on now?

"They convicted Shin for murdering his partner down in Orange County a couple of years back."

"Shin is Asian, right?" I asked.

Bud nodded. "You think that makes a difference to me?"

"Malik, our Indian friend, is south Asian."

"That's a coincidence," Bud said. "Shin's dead partner was a white guy, like Jacob Christian in our case. They never found the body, but the DA convicted Shin. Good trick, right?"

Bud got up, unstrapped his mask, and went to the open window. "This is right out of Shin's playbook. They say he disappeared his partner for money and sent phony emails to his family to make them think the partner was surfing around the world. Gave him a fake girlfriend to travel with. Malik is pulling that same con. His partner sailing the seas with some foreign chick."

Right off the deep end.

"Hey, Mel," I said. "When you get a chance, would you check into the *sinister* Mr. Malik and their company finances." I pretended to curl a long mustache to emphasize *sinister*.

Mel rolled her eyes, pretending I wasn't funny. "I'm leaving early today, remember?" She walked to the door and turned halfway toward us, hand on her hip. "While you two were BS-ing I checked on his credit. Jacob Christian who's a partner in Sir Jacob Antiquities. There's no record of him before 2001, when he showed up in Alaska and then California. No Social Security number, no credit cards." She gave me a self-satisfied smile and eased the door closed behind her. I jotted a couple of notes and put the paper on Mel's desk with a heading, "Questions about Jake Christian." I followed Bud out the door. "If Mel finds records of Jake's travel, we can wrap this up tomorrow."

"He's dead as an Egyptian mummy," Bud said.

CHAPTER 13

JEFF

1991, OKLAHOMA

Jeff's disappointment after their rejection by Reverend Love faded, and his mother didn't mention Jeff's shortcomings again.

After her performance with Reverend Love, parishioners in their church, who used to avoid Jeff's mother, now sought her spiritual advice. Over Pastor Garner's objections, she was placed on the Church Council. She spoke to the congregation that Sunday about her personal love for Christ. And the next Sunday, and the next. The reverend sulked as he watched her, before providing his own disappointing sermons.

Back home, his mother, buoyed by her new popularity, spoke to Jeff lovingly, as she had about Jesus in the church! She called him "exceptional" and "beloved." Jeff wondered if the way she loved him, the way he adored her, was precisely the way Momma felt about Jesus or the way Jesus felt about his Father, Which Art in Heaven.

"The reverend is weak," his momma said. "He'll let us do what we want. When you step up with me, smile down on your brothers and sisters in the congregation. Think of how it would be to give the sermon yourself, and someday you will. We're going to drive that weasel out of the church. We will compel these people to appreciate their Savior."

Sarah hired a tutor, Mr. Jasper, with gray hair and hunched shoulders, who wore button-down plaid shirts and who never failed to mention his thirty years teaching at a bible school in New Orleans. He taught Jeff public speech, bible study, and charismatic preaching. Science was not discussed; math, an after-thought.

Though Jeff wasn't in school with the other kids, he kept one friend. He was pretty sure his mother didn't know about Robbie, who was a couple of years older—almost eleven—with curly brown hair. Robbie wore blue jeans all the time and striped tee shirts. He taught Jeff stuff his mom wouldn't like, about girls and what men and women did in private, swear words too. Robbie knew all about the different makes of cars, transmissions and horsepower. And about growing up.

"Don't call your mother, *Momma*. That's little kid talk."

"She wants me to call her that."

"Don't be a sissy. Call her *mam*, like a grown up."

Some afternoons the boys rode their bikes into the country. Other days they spent time in Robbie's family workshop out behind the garage. The building was big enough to store supplies for the family and also for Robbie's model train setup and a bench where the boys played with his Erector set. The two of them would sit on stools, constructing trucks, or airplanes, or different types of buildings out of the metal parts.

One day when they'd just completed a windmill, they plugged in the Erector set motor and set the sails turning.

Robbie grinned. "Just like in Holland."

"Today we'll grind some corn in the mill," Jeff said. "And tomorrow wheat."

Robbie added, "Maybe we'll hook it up to a generator and make electricity."

"That's a great idea. Is that even possible? Let's unscrew all the pieces tomorrow and build … a carousel," Jeff said.

It was quiet for a moment. Jeff saw Robbie staring at his gloved hand. He'd caught Robbie glancing at it before, but neither one of them had said anything about it.

"You always wear that glove," Robbie said. "Makes me curious."

Jeff slipped his hand under the table. He felt his heart thumping in his chest. "It's nothing."

"Then you can show me," Robbie said.

He couldn't look his friend in the eye.

"Sorry," Robbie said. "I didn't mean nothin' bad."

Jeff had never shown anyone. Only his mother had seen. Robbie was a good guy, and he really didn't mean anything, did he? Slowly, Jeff brought his hand out. He removed his glove and let Robbie see the scar on the back.

"Cool," Robbie said. "I like it."

Which made Jeff laugh. He stripped the bandage off his palm, revealing the irregular welt at its center. Jeff had poked it hard that morning to quench the itch, which made the flesh show dark pink, even here in the dim light of Robbie's shed.

"Ni-i-i-i-ce," Robbie enthused. "Why you want to hide that?"

"My mom doesn't want me to show it." He took in a breath and added. "She says that Jesus had the same thing on his hand."

"Jesus!" Robbie said. "So friggin' cool."

"Friggin'? What's that?"

"It's what you say when you can't say that bad word. If you went to school, like the rest of us, you'd know all this stuff."

"Oh, yeah. Anyway, Momma—Mom— says this one hole's not good enough to make me holy."

Robbie laughed. "Holes make you holy; that's a good one."

Jeff laid both his hands on the work table, revealing the other, unblemished, palm.

"Jesus had lots of holes, one on each hand and each foot. And that cut on his side."

"Holy shit."

Jeff knew what "shit" meant, but he would never say it. "Sometimes I feel bad that I disappoint M-Mom."

"She sounds a little daffy," Robbie said.

Jeff reached over and poked Robbie's shoulder, poked it a second time, harder.

"Don't you dare say that. She's the best."

Robbie gave him a narrow-eyed look, like he might decide to push Jeff off his stool and wail on him. "Okay, I won't say nothin' like that."

"Won't say *anything*." Jeff corrected.

"Yeah, sure."

That night, Jeff thought back to Robbie's words and back to the way his mom always admired the wound on his hand, the way she prodded it … and the blood. "Daffy," Robbie had said. —A word that Jeff understood mainly because it was the name of a cartoon duck.

TWO DAYS LATER they were building the Erector carousel, when Robbie looked at Jeff's hand again.

"I've thought over what you said, 'bout your mam and Jesus."

Jeff felt a nervous flutter in his stomach. Was Robbie going to pick on his mother again?

"Ever wanted to put a hole in the other hand?" Robbie asked. "To make your *mam* proud?"

Jeff cringed. "This hurt really bad when I got it. It itches all the time."

Robbie leaned over from the next stool and laid a hand on Jeff's arm. "What if there's another way, a way that would make you closer to God?" Robbie, being older and going to public school, knew lots of confusing stuff.

"What are you talking about?"

Robbie unplugged the Erector set motor, opened a drawer beneath the table top and removed a cord with a plug on one end and two bare copper wires on the other. "See? Electricity." He plugged it into the wall behind the table and tapped the two bare wires together. It sparked and gave a sound like a whip cracking. Jeff almost jumped off his stool. He didn't see what his friend had in mind, and he wasn't sure he wanted to, but Robbie seemed excited about his idea. Robbie sparked the wires again, and this time Jeff didn't jump.

"You know what lightning is?" Robbie asked.

"Yeah."

"Lightning comes from the sky, like right from God. See? They say when lightning hits people, it marks them on the bottom of their feet."

"Lightning kills people, Robbie."

"This isn't like that. It's only house electricity." Again, Robbie tapped the wires. He grinned and each time he made that spark, he seemed to relish it a little more. "If I put one of these—" He held one wire apart from the other. "—on the back of your hand and one in the front, it'll give you like lightning power, energy from heaven."

Jeff was shaking his head thinking that Robbie was maybe a bit inconsistent in what he was saying.

"It'll make your hands match. Your mam will be over the moon."

What would it be like to have matching scars? What would his mom think? *Over the moon.*

Jeff pictured her smiling that special way she reserved for his best achievements, like when he'd speak a verse from the holy book just right. Maybe it wouldn't hurt that much.

Before Jeff could think more about it and scare himself, he held up his hand. Robbie moved in fast with the wires. A tingling ran through Jeff's hand and up his arm. He yelped and snatched it back, as the tingle turned to a jolt.

Robbie grasped his hand and inspected it. "How was it?"

Jeff was considering just that question. At the first instant he'd felt almost tickled, but then it had really hurt. He examined his palm, where a little patch was turning red.

Robbie moved in close to stare. "Doesn't look like much. Want another one?"

Thinking of his mother and how this might please her, thinking that he could stand to do it once more, just once, he held up his hand. "I'll keep it still this time. Give me a good burn."

IT DIDN'T TAKE LONG for Jeff's mom to notice that he was hiding his left hand. She followed him into his room. "Show me."

Jeff held it out for her. "It's just a little burn."

"How'd you get it?"

There was no way he could tell her about Robbie now. "I did it for you, Momma."

She didn't look mad. She even smiled a little, as she led him into the bathroom to slather his hand with Vaseline and wrap it in gauze.

"Good boy," she said. "This is *excellent*."

CHAPTER 14

STAN

October 2020, Los Angeles

I met Hannah's son, Luke, outside the three-story, brick history building at Brinkman College. He was waiting for me at the top of the stairs out front; tall, around 6-5, with brown hair down to his shoulders.

"Luke?"

"Yeah. Don't come close."

I stopped halfway up. "Like I said on the phone, your mom's worried about your dad."

"Twin assholes." He descended the stairs and started across the lawn. "I told you, I don't want to talk about this." I thought he might bolt on me, but he let me keep up. "What will it take to get rid of you?"

"Tell me if you've heard from your dad."

He slapped at a bug that was buzzing near his ear. "Got an email last night. Some coincidence you showing up the next day." Clearly, he didn't believe it was. "Third time he's written in the last month."

"Give me a copy and tell me why you're mad at them."

He glared at me.

"Don't run," I said. "Or I'll come back tomorrow, find out what classes you're in and sit beside you."

"I could deck you."

"You're big, but you're not a jock. I have Army training."

Luke gave out a little snort. "I walked in on my father and some naked bitch in our living room. She had honkin'-good boobs, and she wasn't in a hurry to cover them. That was before my mother kicked him out."

"She know about the woman?"

"Don't think so. They've had a shit relationship for years."

"Print me off a copy of that last email, and I'll leave you alone."

I waited outside Luke's dorm building, as he printed it. We stood ten feet apart on the lawn, while I read it.

Hi Luke

I know we've had a hard time lately, but please know that I love you. I understand your mother's worried about me, but I'm all right. Actually doing better than I have in a while. My relationship with your mom has been hard. I know it's taken a toll on us, but you're still my son. Please remember that.

I guess I've failed in many ways. I'd like to make it up to you. I promise to try, but right now I have to be on my own a bit. I'll be away on business a while. I need time. I really need time. Please tell your mother not to worry. Tell her I regret many things. I'm just not up to answering her questions right now. She always asked so many doggone questions. I'll be in touch when I get back to the States. Not sure how soon that will be.

Love

Dad

"That sound like your father?" I asked.

"Hell no. He'd never say he failed … and who the fuck says 'doggone?'"

"Tell your mom about the emails?"

He shook his head.

"Why not?"

"She's only pretending to worry."

Poor little rich kid.

CHAPTER 15

BUD

Stan called and asked me to meet him at his house. It's a brown and white ranch-style in a pretty good neighborhood. The garage door was open, and I found Stan in there fiddling with something at his work bench. We leaned against the side of his white Escape, as I read Luke Christian's email.

"This is more buffalo shit, Stan. You gotta see it."

"Maybe but—"

"I'm going with you to get Hannah's take on this."

"I don't think …" Stan had that uncertain look of his.

"You're not competent to judge, my friend. You think she's oh-so-sweet, but she's phony as a five-dollar Rolex."

"And you're hung up on this Ed Shin thing of yours."

"We all have our own illusions, partner." Hannah's virgin charms being one of his. Maybe the Ed Shin thing was one of mine, but I didn't think so. "Take me to see Hannah, and we'll get her talking."

Stan had his cheek puffed out and his mouth sideways, ready to turn me down.

"Come on, Stan; this is criminal investigation 101. Never question a suspect by yourself, when you want to fuck her."

"Straight from the detective manual?"

"You got it."

He shook his head, grinning. "I must be nuts."

We climbed into the Escape, our usual positions.

"We're all nuts, Stanley," I said. "Now, James, you may drive me to our destination. On the way I'll tell you my latest revelation from the internet."

"Great." Stan pulled away from the curb. He made fun of the little factoids I provided, but I knew he loved them.

"This doctor has a video on YouTube; it's all over the web. He's the real thing, wearing a stethoscope and one of those mirror things strapped to his forehead."

"Totally credible," Stan said.

"He's actually a *professor*—proctology, I think. Turns out this baby was born with his nuts growing in his armpits."

Stan laughed. "A proctologist would be more about butts than balls." He braked to avoid a kid on bicycle that swerved into the street.

I rolled down my window and yelled, "Be careful, you little shit."

Stan was still laughing about the proctologist. "You'd have to be careful with your testicles up there. Swing a baseball bat and … *Ouch.*"

"I guess. The interesting thing was that the baby's right nut wound up in his left armpit and his left nut in the right armpit."

"How could they tell?" Stan asked. "Do baby's testicles have L and R stenciled on them, like H and C on water faucets?"

This felt great; teasing each other, laughing it up like we used to.

"You don't believe that story yourself," Stan said.

"You never know with me, partner." I liked to keep Stan guessing, but he played along. That was part of what I loved about our friendship.

AT HER FRONT DOOR, Hannah gave Stan a sweet smile.

She soured up when she spotted me. "Ug."

She actually said, "Ug!" I loved it.

She wore an expensive-looking pantsuit, pale blue. She pouted for Stan, and we all headed to her living room. Hannah landed herself in the armchair.

Stan handed her Luke's email and took his old spot on the sofa. "Your husband sent this to your son. There were a couple before this."

I wandered around, like I had the other day, picking up a statue and examining it, then a trophy, doing my best to distract her from sending I-need-you eyes at my partner. I grabbed a fancy vase.

She set Luke's email on the mermaid table.

I tucked the vase under one arm and snatched up a picture of Jake Christian with his son holding fishing poles—two dweebs in floppy hats. "Your dear Jake's abandoned you, and your son's pissed, right? Or maybe that email's a fake. What do you think, Hannah-babe?"

Stan looked peeved, but he didn't interfere. Maybe he was thinking over what I'd said before.

She scowled. "Jake and Luke had an issue. Neither one would discuss it. So Jake might write something like this."

I set the vase and the picture on the table, slipped Jake's email to Malik from my pocket and handed it to her. "How about Jake, the explorer with his new Indian chick, sailing the Indian Ocean?"

"Crap, Bud." Stan looked mad, but, obviously, she needed to see this.

Hannah's eyes teared up as she read. She straightened and took in air. "He's making it sound like I pestered him, but *he's* the one who always wanted to see *me* after we separated."

"You and your husband have a prenup?" I asked.

Hannah looked to Stan for help, but he just stared at the floor. She gave me the old nasty eye. "You think I would …"

"Of course not." I put on a phony grin. "How many lawyers do you and Mr. Christian employ?" Hannah was still giving Stan the wounded-girl come-on. Funny, except Stan was looking at her again, and he was the type to swallow her act.

"All right, here's the truth. My husband is a goddamn liar. His partner too, but Malik's vile, and Jake's just …"

"Do you think that's real?" Stan asked.

"I can believe an affair. Sure I can. But Jake always made fun of that ass, Malik. He'd never share something this personal with him." She eyed the paper again. "And he isn't the campy, outdoor type. He wouldn't sleep on a sailboat, even for a night. He wouldn't be this spontaneous."

She took in another long breath, looked at me, and said, "You showed me this to hurt me. Is that fun for you?" She gave Stan a sideways screw-you look. "And you did nothing to help." She stood and pointed toward the door. "Get out now, both of you."

I could see that Stan wanted to apologize, but he didn't.

We went outside and stood on the sidewalk by the Escape. I pretended to puff on a cigar. "If I smoked, I'd light up a stogie to celebrate that interrogation."

Stan started pacing. "Inquisition's more like it."

"You didn't stop me, because …"

"Yeah," he said. "Okay, I guess you needed to push it a little."

Another puff on my pretend stogie. "You should thank me, Stan. I wanted to ask her about the stigmata. That would have been juicy, but I thought she'd had enough."

"You *are* a sensitive guy," he said. "That hurt Hannah, you know."

Looked like it had hurt Stan too.

"Crocodile tears," I said. "We got some really good info."

"What's that?"

"She confirms my theory. Those emails are fake. Sirjay made them up."

"Maybe. You take the car. Go follow up on the Sturgis case. I'm going back to apologize."

CHAPTER 16

STAN

When Hannah answered the door, she took my breath away. She'd changed into a white terrycloth romper. (That's what Cheryl used to call them.) Bare shoulders and bare legs. My fingers were tempted to trace her collar bones.

It had only been a few minutes since she threw us out, but she didn't look upset.

"I came back to make up with you," I said.

She gave me a look. "Make up? We're not friggin' kids. Why the hell did you bring Bud?"

"He has a theory about your husband, and ..."

She looked into my eyes, in that old way that disarmed me. "What is it? You can tell me."

"I can't."

She crossed her arms in front of her, looking grumpy. Back and forth, sour and sweet and sour. What was Hannah doing?

"It's only an idea," I said.

"Screw him, Stan. Bud's a damned fool."

Good point.

"You think those emails prove my husband's all right, but none of this is like him, and it's pissing me off."

The thing was that I was starting to worry about Jake's safety too, especially now that Hannah seemed to be channeling Bud's theory. She was counting on me to find him. She looked up at me, hazel eyes trusting me, prettier than my last girlfriend, Anna, or Cheryl, for that matter.

I pushed a lock of hair off her face. "We're still friends?"

She gave a tentative smile. "How about a swim? I was going to go nude. I can stick with that plan or put on a suit. You can use one of Jake's."

Damn, that was tempting.

It was one of those October days in Southern California, when the Santa Ana winds heated things up. I flashed back on our nude swim all those years back, but nude would be a mistake. Hannah was a client. We'd have to wear bathing suits, but then I thought, *My privates floating in a dead man's trunks.*

"No thanks."

"Okay, we'll just talk."

She led me out to the patio and we lay on a two-person lounger. I turned on my side, looking Hannah over.

She gave me a minute and then said, "You're staring."

"Admiring. Your body's even better. Sorry, I shouldn't—"

"Better than what?"

"You remember the night of our prom?"

"Mmmm. You got a really good look at me that night."

"In the moonlight at Harry's Pond. I was so turned on. I'd never hugged a naked girl."

"We did everything but … That was my first too," she said.

"First?"

"Orgasm with a guy. You got jumpy when I screamed for joy."

We laughed, and she pushed me on my back. She slid next to me, with her back against my side, her head on my shoulder, my arm wrapped across her chest. It felt Covid safe that way, not breathing on each other. And very exciting. "It's great being with you," she said. "I've felt abandoned."

There was no way Hannah would harm her husband, no way she'd lie to me now that we were getting close again. Waves of nostalgia and lust washed over me. I stroked along her side, feeling her enticing breasts beneath my arm. Without warning, that feeling of despair slipped into my heart, despair from twenty years back when I found out she'd had sex with another guy. I felt her ribs with my fingers, focusing on this moment, crowding out the old hurt. Trying, anyway.

She's married. She's a client. "I'd better go," I said.

"Hey, Stan. Come on. Don't you like feeling me up?"

"I like it too much, Hannah." I freed myself and stood.

Anger flashed in her eyes, as she got up. But it faded to regret by the time we reached the front door. She wanted what I wanted. —Obvious, but we had to resist.

"I'll find Jake," I said.

"I know you will, Stan, and promise me—" Her eyes narrowed. "—if he's doing something wrong, you have to tell me."

Later, at home, I pictured the moonlight glinting off the pond twenty-one years back; her silhouette, the way she'd been all-but naked, kissing her, caressing, the soft dark curls of her hair blowing across her face in the breeze, the silvery skin of her thighs and buttocks as she slipped off her underpants and dove into the water. If we'd made love that night, everything might be different now.

CHAPTER 17

BUD

Stan and Mel were at their desks, when I bopped in around ten that next morning. I stopped in the doorway, checking them out. Stan was my friend, and Mel was now too. She was beginning to *blossom* lately. —There's a word no one would expect from me. She wore those big glasses and an emerald green mask that looked fine with her skin tone. She got up from her desk, moved over by the open window, and removed the mask. She was pretty, and she clearly liked Stan. He was blind as a starfish. While he mooned over a devious bitch ex-girlfriend, here was a really nice, single babe ready to jump in his lap. *Chowderhead* was the good old-fashioned name for my partner—another one of those words.

"Glad you're here," Mel said. "Now I can tell you both the latest. You know the missing financial records for Jacob Christian before 2001; there are no school records either. His resumé says he went to Whitney High and has a marketing degree from Penn State. The internet begs to differ." She glanced at her computer screen and back at Stan. "The internship at Clark Brokerage— bogus. I called the company. Which makes your missing dude technically a *ghost*."

Stan rolled his desk chair halfway between Mel and me. "Were you able to check on his travel?"

"No info yet," she said. "By the way, his emails were routed through a server in Phnom Penh, Cambodia. God knows where they originated."

"Why would Jake Christian do that?" Stan asked.

I plopped into a chair at the table. "Jake-boy wants to escape from Hannah-girl. He doesn't have the balls to tell her, and doesn't want her to know where he is. Pretends to be on a business trip, or ..." I held up a beat to make sure I had their attention. "They're phony emails from an Unsub who ripped Jake Christian's body to shreds and threw him down a well."

"I like that." Mel winked at me. Melanie and I both loved TV crime dramas. I'd sprout a theory, and Mel would jump on the bandwagon, or visa-versa. I would have asked Mel out, but she had too much class for me, not to mention a few inches in height.

Stan was laughing, the way he did when Mel and I played together like that.

Mel moved back to her computer and began typing.

"If this ghost appeared in 2001, we should check out a 9-11 angle," I said.

Melanie didn't bother to look up from her computer. "Sure, Bud. Go check that out. See if he had a pilot's license."

Stan was still chuckling. "I thought you hated Hannah Christian. Now you want to—what? —dedicate your life to her case?"

I leaned back in my chair. "It's no longer about that skank. It's about her husband and his partner. It's about murdering a guy, disposing of him and sending fake emails to his partner—who is also the murderer—and to his son."

"Yeah," Stan said. "Just like that case you've been raving about."

I gave him a triumphant fist shake. "Ed Shin, convicted of killing his partner. Sending sham emails, just like this."

Over at her desk, Mel waved at us. "I just got a message from their supplier in India, the one Jacob Christian was supposed to visit two weeks ago."

"I bet he never showed," I said. "Right?"

Mel looked a little deflated. "Right, Bud. Mr. Christian ordered the new merchandise over the internet."

"Or that Indian crap-merchant, Malik, placed the order. Like I've been sayin', it's that Indian prick all the way. We've got to search that bastard's store, like they did in the Ed Shin case. We'll find blood, sure as shit. We'll confiscate Malik's computer. You and me, partner, making investigative history."

Stan gave me one of his looks and jabbed a finger my way. "Not *we*, and not *partner*. If you do that, you are not with S. Stein Investigations."

Stan was just being Stan, so damned up-tight. As usual, leaving me to save the day. If searching Sir Jacob Antiquities didn't pan out, my other ideas might.

That 9-11 angle was totally worth a look.

CHAPTER 18

JEFF

Oklahoma, New Mexico, 1993-4

The red electrical burns on Jeff's left hand turned black. The hand throbbed from time to time, but the burned spot had gone numb. His mother kissed it with a tenderness that delighted him, before she slathered makeup on the backs of his hands and the palm of the left. The right palm, still raw from regular gouging, required a proper bandage.

Sarah Lamb kept preaching at their little church, her sermons ever more passionate. Jeff accompanied her to the altar to call out biblical passages. The congregation was in her thrall. Reverend Garner grew despondent. His sermons, that followed hers, shrank. "Sad little tidbits," Jeff's mom called them. As Jeff and his mom greeted parishioners after church, people murmured her praise. Some glanced at the Reverend and rolled their eyes. "He's useless," Jeff's mom said, privately. "He needs to go, but what other parish will have him?"

One Sunday, Jeff noticed a conspicuous stranger in church, a man with neatly-styled brown hair, wearing an elegant navy-blue suit. The pews weren't quite full, but this guy chose to stand by a side wall. All of that caught Jeff's attention. Most remarkable was the fellow's build; brawny, like a football lineman.

The service ended. The man remained off to the side, as Jeff and his mom chatted with their brethren. Finally, he approached. Jeff was sure his mom saw the man coming, but she didn't look at him.

The big man said, "Good day, Mrs. Lamb. I'm Bob Smithfield."

She turned toward him and flashed a dazzling smile.

"I'm on the board of several churches around the south, many in Florida. It's my pleasure to arrange guest appearances for visiting preachers."

"I've heard of you, Mr. Smithfield," his mom said. "Yes, I have."

"We've heard of you too Mrs. Lamb, all the way over in Palm Beach. I've come all this way to hear you, and I'm very glad I did."

His mother blushed, took the hand the big man offered and held it for a moment.

Smithfield kissed the back of her hand. "You have a bright future, dear lady."

"Why, thank you, Mr. Smithfield." She looked fondly at him for maybe half a minute. "I've been waiting for a new sign from God, Mr. Smithfield, and your visit may be just that."

She glanced at Jeff. "Jeff, show Mr. Smithfield your gift."

Jeff's hands shook a little, as he held them out.

His mom gave an exasperated snort. "Remove the glove, *son*." As Jeff pulled it off, she reached in her handbag and produced a tissue. "Now clean the other palm."

Jeff wiped the makeup off his left hand, as best he could, and showed Smithfield the blackened palm.

"Jeff's wounds were the first signs God provided, Mr. Smithfield."

The big man grinned. "Mrs. Lamb, I believe we can parlay this into something." He winked. "Something quite rewarding."

His mom nodded toward the exit. "Jeff, dear, Mr. Smithfield and I could use some privacy."

Feeling a bit hurt, Jeff went outside and waited on a boulder across the street from the little church. When the two of them emerged a half hour later, Smithfield seemed pleased, Jeff's mom, elated.

SARAH LAMB HAD ALLIES in the church now, parishioners who put pressure on Reverend Garner and the church trustees.

Bob Smithfield worked with amazing speed, finding a congregation down in Mississippi that would take Garner. The reverend accepted his fate and departed with barely a whimper.

Sundays now belonged to Sarah Lamb.

On weekdays, Mr. Jasper, the tutor drove him and his mom into the deserted countryside and commanded Jeff to unleash the power of his voice. His mother encouraged and critiqued.

At the pulpit, they both wore white gloves, raising their hands high and praising Jesus. They called on their brethren to roar His holy name. Jeff led them with shouts of, "Praise the Lord," and "Alleluia." The congregation's fervent responses exhilarated him.

People from nearby towns overflowed the pews. Bob Smithfield arrived with a couple of men in high class suits. The three men huddled with Jeff's mom in private.

SEVERAL MONTHS AFTER she'd assumed the ministry, over toast and jam in their plain kitchen, Jeff's mother patted him on the cheek and announced: "The church can do without us for a couple of weeks. We're going to the cabin."

Did she mean *the cabin*?

They hadn't been to New Mexico in six years, since his father died in a boating accident just after Jeff's fourth birthday. The modest two room dwelling sat at the far end of a dirt road, atop a mesa on the edge of Navajo country. Their neighbors, all Navajo, lived in the traditional round or octagonal wooden *hogans*, others in simple box-like houses. Pinion pines dotted the slopes. Sheep grazed.

Images of that landscape and those native people evoked a vague wonder in Jeff. Memories flitted in his thoughts: exploring canyons and mesas with his dad, wandering dry washes where streams had cut through, exposing layers of stone.

His father, Byron Little, sold insurance, but he dreamed of finding mineral wealth to free him from that dreary work. He'd acquired the cabin as a base for exploration, because uranium permeated the land as far as the eye could see. Byron Little wasn't a geologist, but he believed that uranium had to coexist with more lucrative minerals.

Rather than gold or silver, he discovered sandstone and sagebrush. Yet, even after weeks of futile exploration, at the end of each exhausting day, Jeff's father would point to an unexplored canyon and say, "Look, son; another fine prospect for tomorrow." And Jeff would anxiously await the next sun rise.

"Great," Jeff said to his mother now. "What will we do there for fun?"

"We hike. We commune with nature. We get ourselves right with God and Jesus."

Jeff *already* spent every day, with his mom and his tutor, *getting right with Jesus.*

"This will be our retreat, son, where we prepare to launch our ministry. You want that, don't you? Our ministry?"

Reliving his exhilaration when the people shouted, *Alleluia*, he said, "Of course, Momma."

"You'll love this, Jeff. We'll go over to Monument Valley in Utah. That's a special place, like a vision of God's creation. We'll hike into the wilderness where we can shout our love of Jesus to the heavens, because you are going to preach with me. You will become one terrific orator, Jeffrey Lamb, and your hands; we will transform them. Your hands will heal people ... and convince them."

Jeff prayed sometimes that his father's perseverance and his mother's strength would bolster his own shabby spirit. Then he could be the boy she wanted. He could preach with her. He could!

THEY STOPPED FOR SUPPLIES at a supermarket in Grants NM, and then drove the last sixty miles to the cabin. Jeff was amazed to see that old place—so small! Unpainted wood, with a tarpaper roof.

The door creaked, as they entered, carrying some of their belongings. Inside there was one large room—a living room, kitchen, workspace—one small bedroom, and a bathroom. His mom unpacked a picture of Jesus, preaching on the Mount and set it on a shelf where Christ could watch over them. Jeff opened windows and threw back the shutters, while his mom wiped dust off the counter. They brought in groceries and poured ice into the back of the ice box.

When everything had been stowed, she summoned Jeff to sit with her at the scratched, yellow Formica table. "You know we don't drink liquor," she said, looking him in the eye.

Her intensity worried him a little, and he thought for a second about Reverend Love and his whiskey. "Uh huh."

"We don't fornicate or curse. We don't take His name in vain."

"Yes, Mom."

"*Momma*, Jeff. I like you to call me *Momma*. Now repeat after me, 'Whiskey is the devil's drink.'"

Jeff did as he was told.

"I bought liquor back in Grants." She reached into the bag that sat on the floor beside her and brought out a small, clear bottle, *Vodka*, and a jug of orange juice. "Tonight, just this one time, we imbibe for God's purpose." That shocked him … thrilled him a little too.

She brought a bowl of ice from the icebox. She added ice to two glasses and filled one half-way with the clear liquid. She looked at him for a long time, her eyes regretful and then poured orange juice into both. Jeff's drink tasted a little funny but not that different from normal juice. She watched him, as she poured another drink. Soon Jeff felt a little queasy and very silly.

"Funny. I feel funny."

So, this was how the devil tempted people. But why was Mom doing this? For God's purpose, she'd said.

"We're going to do an experiment." She brought out some dishtowels and a sharp little knife. He watched with amused curiosity, as she cleaned the knife with Vodka. She took Jeff's left hand, the one with a black burned patch, and poked the palm with her knuckle. "Feel anything?"

"No, Mom."

She held his hand tighter, without a word, and gave it a quick jab with the knife. He jerked back and looked first at his mother and then at the blood dribbling out of him. "Why'd you do that?"

Her face was close. She appeared a little blurry after the funny orange juice. "Did it hurt, son? I don't want to hurt you."

"That part of my hand never hurts, no matter what." He watched the pretty red droplets falling onto the yellow table. "Does this make me like Jesus?"

"Yes, son. You are very much like Him." She seized his hand about to stab again.

The color might be pretty, but this was gross too … scary.

Jeff stared at the oozing slit in his palm, saw the flash of the blade's quick thrust, a new spirt.

Blood flying out of me! This isn't funny. It's disgusting. She's given me alcohol! Devil's drink! He ripped his hand away and jumped up. "What are you doing, mother?"

She gazed up at him, surprised. "Why, I'm making you perfect, Jeffrey."

He stumbled outside, as she shouted something he didn't comprehend. He ran along the rim of the mesa and down into a canyon.

Jeff woke in the dirt, face gritty, the side of his throbbing head resting on a flat rock. His shoulder and hip ached. A puddle of squashed puke lay beside him. He must have rolled in it!

His head filled up with weird thoughts. –Vodka, his mother attacking him like a mad assassin. He sat up and looked at his left hand, a bloody, filthy wound at the center. Holy God, could it be true?

He staggered uphill. When he reached the top of the mesa, he heard his mother calling. "Jeff. Jeff." –Her voice hoarse.

"Mom!"

They met not far from the cabin. She grabbed his hand and stared at it. "*Jeff*, now look what you've done." She took him inside, tweezed a few slivers of stone out of his palm and scrubbed it hard. –Good thing he'd lost all sense in it.

"Why did you run, son?"

His thoughts dull, his hand numb, and its wound revolting; he could only stare at her.

"You wanted this, Jeff. You wanted to be like Him."

She was right. He had, after all, let Robbie zap him with that electric cord. But he didn't want it this bad.

"This is vital for our ministry, Jeff. We'll reveal your bloody hands, and they'll all believe. You want to save people, don't you?"

He did want to save people, bring them to Jesus, but he didn't want to be a freak, the way he'd been when the boys mocked him. "*Jeffy, you throw like a girl.*" Imagine what they'd shout if he was the boy with bleeding hands!

"No, mother, we don't have to. That would be a lie."

It took a few days and many recriminations. *Jeff, you're not dedicated enough; Jeff, you disappoint me; Jeff, this is what Jesus wishes; Jeff, Mr. Smithfield and I have discussed this, and—*

The Jesus argument almost convinced him, but, when she brought up Smithfield, it steeled his resolve. "Stop it, Mother. Mr. Smithfield isn't a nice man."

Finally, his mother relented. "Here's what we'll do," she said. "We will go onstage and preach. We'll both wear gloves. You will touch people and heal them. I will tell them you have God's wounds, but you won't have to show them."

"I can't heal people."

"You can, son. You'll see."

He took a deep breath. "If we tell them I have wounds, they'll want to see them."

"Then—"

"We won't tell them about the wounds. I don't want—"

She brushed the hair back from his forehead, and scrutinized him for a long minute. "Okay, son, we won't tell them."

She would never lie to him, so he agreed.

They stayed at the cabin several more days, driving up to the mountains in Colorado a couple of times and to Canyon de Chelly to hike down to the shells of old rock homes of the Anasazi, the ancient people. Those places filled him with wonder, as did Window Rock, where his mom said God had pierced the stone cliff with His mighty, swift sword, just as He had pierced Jeff's hands.

BACK IN OKLAHOMA, Bob Smithfield stopped by and took Jeff's mom for a three hour "business lunch".

When she returned, she announced. "We're on the move, son. Bob's arranging for us to preach in some really grand churches. We'll share the Word with so many souls!"

Thrilling news. If only someone besides Smithfield had arranged it.

She ordered a white robe for herself and a white suit for him. She wrapped Jeff's left hand in gauze. —It was still oozing. They both donned gloves before preaching at a cathedral all the way over in Florida, then a huge church in Montgomery, and later to a congregation in Kansas. She unleashed orations, confident and strong, like she'd been that night when Reverend Love came to town. She held Jeff's hands high and announced to those worshippers: "This is my remarkable boy, Jeff. He has healing hands. Come to Baton Rouge on Easter Sunday and you'll find out how amazing he is."

After each service, men and women crowded close around, beaming and praising his mom's strength. Some brought little children, encouraging them to touch Jeff's clothing. Meeting the people, he reminded himself over and over, *I have to look happy. I have to look confident and holy. Momma wants me to.*

SPIRITUAL LIGHT SHONE in her eyes, as she washed and wrapped his hands one evening. "On Easter, Jeff, you're going to read the gospel of resurrection very loud and very strong, the way you do for me and Mr. Jasper. Then you will heal them, as Jesus did. Okay?"

"But how?"

"We will show them how holy you are, just like our Lord. You *will* heal people."

"I don't … we can't."

"Mr. Smithfield will help us, son. He'll have people there who are ready to be cured."

"Ready? How does he know?"

"Don't worry. You'll be able."

Confusing. "They'll know I'm not the Lord."

"We're not trying to fool them, as much as to help them. God wants us to do this, because …" She stopped to think a moment. "Some people are plain ignorant. We're going to trick them to do the right thing."

"Why would God make them ignorant?"

"He's testing us, son, to see if we're true and faithful. To see if *we* are strong."

For God, he could bear this.

That Easter, they performed their first "Miracle Sunday." The audience gasped on cue. People he touched, all but a few, abandoned their crutches and wheelchairs and walked again. Amazing!

Jeff had just turned eleven.

CHAPTER 19

STAN

I read over the email from Jake Christian's suppliers in India, saying that they hadn't seen him lately. I checked out their websites. The pictures looked like a tour through Sir Jacob Antiquities. It would be easy for Christian—or Malik for that matter—to order this stuff online and have it shipped. Bud's theories, and Mel's revelations fueled my suspicions. I asked Mel to see if she could find out who placed the orders.

I had another question, too. I rolled my chair over, coming to a stop a safe distance away from her. "You don't think Bud would really break into Malik's place?"

"Not a chance." She flashed a grin, took off her glasses and set them on her desk. "He's such a levelheaded fellow." She seldom looked straight at me for more than a few moments, but this time she did, which made me feel a little shy.

She glanced at the glasses in her hand. "I don't always need these." I was getting a better look. Melanie's face was like milk-chocolate shaped from an appealing mold. Not the cheekbones of a model. Not beautiful, or maybe she was, a little. Did she realize how good this small bit of intimacy felt to me?

"If I wasn't black, you'd see me blush," she said.

"Sorry. I didn't mean to …"

"It's all right, Stan. I'm looking at you too."

Gazing into each other's eyes, I ignored my hesitation and plunged. "Hey, Mel, would you like to walk down and get some pizza at Mike's?"

She gave me a brilliant smile. "Heck, yeah." She put the glasses back on, then took them off and popped them into her pocketbook.

We ate sitting at a blue picnic table under palm trees outside Mike's Pizza Pad, speculating about the pedestrians walking by. We talked about TV shows and movies. Melanie liked crime dramas—no surprise there. We laughed about Bud's theories, like his 9-11 gambit.

"He could write for television," she told me. "If he had the drive to sell himself."

"Maybe."

"I've noticed the way you treat Bud."

I expected mockery but didn't find any.

"You're really nice, even when he provokes you." Mel had a sweet, affectionate look in her eyes.

"Guess I'm a sap," I said.

"Totally not. You're that way with everyone, not just with Bud. For instance, you don't get cranky when I make a mistake."

"You're the last person to mess up."

She chuckled. "See what I mean?"

"Thanks, Mel. I try." The compliment made me uneasy. "I guess it's time to go."

We stood, strapped on our masks, and met at the end of the table.

"I wear the glasses to make me feel safe," she said.

"You don't need them?"

She gestured at her eyes. "Twenty-twenty. I've had some bad experiences."

Dying to ask, *does that mean you're not dating anyone?* but not wanting to make her uncomfortable, I went silent.

"I don't seem to need the glasses with you." She looked down. "Well, I'm off to my afternoon job." She didn't budge.

I wanted to hug her really bad. Maybe she wanted that too. Why else stand there waiting?

I stepped forward, turned my head to the side, and we shared a quick embrace. Had that been okay, with me being her boss? It felt nice, innocent, comforting. What was wrong with that?

I stood for a minute on the sidewalk, watching her walk off, feeling warm inside, like I might when I'm twenty pages into a new book—stopping to appreciate the depth and beauty of the writing and mulling intriguing questions that bubbled in my head.

How different this felt from my last visit with Hannah. No offers of nudity. No talk about leaving her alone and lonely. No husband. –I was almost sure.

I'D HAD LUNCH with Mel a couple of times in the year since I'd hired her, but not since Covid had broken out. We'd talked about work, and she'd barely looked at me. This time, she'd opened up a little. –She shared a house with her mother. Her sister and brother-in-law lived just down the block. The drawings behind her computer came from her favorite niece. I'd shied away—and she hadn't offered—answers to other questions, like: What caused her retreat into baggy clothes and glasses she didn't need? Why live with her mom? What sort of woman inhabited the space behind those lenses?

I ARRIVED LATE the next morning with a strawberry Danish for Melanie.

Mel swiveled her chair toward me, took the bag from me, and looked inside. "Nice, thanks."

She wasn't wearing those big, funky glasses, and she whipped off her mask to eat the pastry, filling me in between bites. "No way Jacob Christian was born in Akron, Ohio. I checked with the city clerk, the county clerk and State of Ohio records."

"When did you have time for that?"

"On my other job." She waved what was left of the Danish in the air. "Hey, this is super good."

"You and Bud are really liking this case," I said.

"It beats workers' comp fraud all to heck. By the way, I haven't found any record of Jacob Christian flying to India or Indonesia or anywhere else last month."

Which of course made sense now.

Bud would be out on a surveillance by now, so we called him on the speaker phone. "Hey, Bud," I said. "Mel's got new info."

"Let's have it," he said.

Melanie filled him in about Jake Christian and then said, "See, just like on NCIS—this Christian fellow vaporized into being out of nowhere."

"Yeah, Mel," Bud said. "I like the way you think."

The two of them were about to go off on one of their animated discussions of TV detective shows. I left them to it and walked outside. I sat in the Escape, thinking over nagging questions. Malik might have some of the answers. I called him.

"Sir Jacob Antiquities. Please to appreciate this fine day."

"Mr. Malik, this is Stan Stein. My partner and I came to see you the other day."

There was a pause. "Yes, detective."

"We're checking into Jake Christian, and some of his information doesn't hold up. Did he ever talk about his education?"

"I gave you the resume. What more could you—?"

"The resume is *fake,* Mr. Malik. You spoke with him many times. Did he mention his degree in business administration?"

"That's quite amusing. He appeared very young, when he came to me. His resume said twenty-two years with a business degree, but I came to wonder. His knowledge was—" Malik clucked. "—sadly lacking. I might have dismissed him, but he was a talented salesman. I taught him many, many things about business, very fast, I did. He was bright, and he had a certain quality; almost like a holy man, he was."

"Perhaps your partner made an offhand comment about schooling or a job he'd held." I let the thought hang.

"Well … yes, maybe. Right the first day, I asked if he had sales experience. He said he'd been very fine at selling religion."

"Did he give you more? What religion, or where?"

"Jake was very—is very—closed off. He didn't—doesn't— talk like that way. … Oh, once he did speak of selling religion *to audiences.* Does that help?"

"It does, Mr. Malik. It reminds me too; you said you found Jake talking to the statues in your store about Jesus."

"Yes. Yes. Very strange, if you ask me."

"Yes. Very." I thanked him and hung up.

Pretty good information.

Back inside, Mel was at her computer.

"I really enjoyed lunch with you yesterday," I said.

"Me too." She masked up and came over to me, only a couple of feet apart. Her eyes—I might have imagined it—affectionate. I thought about kissing her on the cheek, mask to mask. It seemed like she might want that too. We both backed up a step.

"Want to do it again?" I asked.

"Can I take a raincheck?" She laid a hand on her stomach. "I'm stuffed."

CHAPTER 20

BUD

Last time Stan and I talked about Trump, Stan called him an "asshole," because Trump refused to wear a protective mask. I would have congratulated Stan for slinging a profanity my way. Instead, I got pissed and clouded his face with Corona breath. It came home to me then how important Trump is to me, important in a personal way. Our president, as usual, is so far out in front of the phony scientists and political shit-heads. Catch it and get over it; that's the way to handle Covid. Boost the economy. Save people's jobs.

While I stand with Trump on the issues, Stan's my main guy. I can't let the arguments get that hot ever again. So I tease and torment him, like we used to do to each other back in the army. I'll throw out something serious, because Stan needs to hear it. Before he contradicts me, I follow up with BS to keep him off balance. I act like Trump is all truth and light, even when he's off base. Bleach in the veins, sure; I've got a gallon of Clorox and a hypodermic under my sink. If Stan mentions nutty theories, like talk that Hillary Clinton rips off children's faces and drinks their blood— "Possible," I say.

Drives him nuts.

Trump accuses the Dems of planning to steal the election. I'd never admit this to my friend, but no one knows if more votes will be stolen for Trump or for Biden. Skepticism works both ways; you have to question your side as well as the opponent's (and maybe even think about what Stan says once in a while). No matter, when Stan claims Trump is "anti-American for downing our democracy," I take Trump's side.

Because deep down I love Stan, and because we can't let the arguments go too far, once in a while, I act like maybe … almost … sort of, I agree with him.

STAN

BUD AND I STOPPED by a taco truck near Baylor Park. I got a veggie burrito and Bud ordered three "Mombo Tacos." Bud had Coke, sparkling water for me. We walked to a picnic table under an oak tree. I'd decided not to tell him about Malik's latest info until I'd had time to think it over. No need to send him into the deep end of conspiracy-land just yet.

After a couple of minutes, for some stupid reason, I thought I'd try to find some common ground with him: "You're not still a disciple of this Q-Anon crud?" This seemed so obvious to me; Bud must have recognized the folly by now. If he could separate some of the nutty crap on the internet from the truth, maybe we'd make progress.

He set a half-eaten taco onto its wrapper and swigged Coke, a bemused smirk on his lips. "I thought you wanted to avoid Trump talk."

"I was foolish and watched ten minutes on Fox last night, and I'm wondering if you—"

Bud, still grinning— "Trump fighting a secret gang of sex perverts and Satanists hiding in the government; you gotta love it."

"That's nuts," I said. "Do people think that? Do you?"

He picked up his taco, took a chomp and spoke with his mouth full. "I'd say ninety percent of it holds water."

I gripped my burrito a little tighter and stared. "Any lunatic can post anything on the internet. It spreads like wildfire. Why even bother with it?"

Still chewing— "I've got a theory: Russian online trolls created Q. They want to blow our democracy up using our own internet."

I thought about that for a few seconds. It almost made sense. There were malevolent forces at play on the internet, no doubt about that.

"Americans are gullible," Bud said. "We grew up on computer games full of monsters and cyborgs, whatever those are."

"People who believe aren't just kids," I said. "Like you, Bud."

"Americans are fools. The Russians have us by the gonads." Bud calling himself a fool? That was a new one. There was a little splat. A white and black mound of bird crud appeared on the table six inches from Bud's elbow. He looked up into the tree and shouted, "Go to hell. –What was I sayin'? You know there's a club on the internet for wacko people who think the world is flat." Bud was being spectacularly reasonable all of a sudden. "Trump really appreciates Q-Anon." He grinned. "He's against pedophilia, just like they are."

So much for lucidity. "Can you be serious for a minute?"

"Serious hasn't worked too well between us, Stan, and I value our friendship." Bud picked up his second taco, still in its wrapper and waved it at me. His mischievous smirk reappeared.

"The Russians love my man, Trump." He unwrapped the taco halfway and pretended to dip it in the bird poop. "But Trump is playing Putin, waiting for an opportunity to screw his ass. I can tell you that story if—"

Just another replay of past frustrations, a damned mistake bringing it up. "Naw, that's enough for now."

CHAPTER 21

BUD

The package from Amazon was waiting on my front steps, when I got home. I brought it inside, opened it and ripped the bubble-wrap away. The spray can said,

Activated Luminol,

Caution,

Flammable,

Breathing Hazard

I stuffed the can, a flashlight, and lock picking device into a fanny pack, but it was way too early. I grilled a burger on the hibachi outside my back door and watched Criminal Minds reruns on TV for a few hours. Around midnight, I put on a black hoody and dark jeans. I drove to a neighborhood behind Sir Jacob Antiquities.

This operation was no big deal. I should have been cool about it, but my heart hammered like a carpenter framing a house. Damn me.

Picking the lock on the back door was easy. I slipped inside and stood breathing slow, finding my bearings.

I made for Jake Christian's office. First Jake's and then Malik's to grab that scumbag's computer; that was the plan. If this murder followed the pattern from Ed Shin's caper, Jake's office would supply the blood evidence.

I ran my flashlight beam around in there. No marks on the walls, nothing along the baseboards. I pulled out the desk, moving it slowly to cut down on noise. In Shin's case, the partner repainted the place to cover the blood spatter. Malik would have too. He'd have replaced the rug, but blood would have seeped into the concrete floor. No blood visible behind the desk, I slid it back in place.

Too much time, this was taking too much time. My watch said only eight minutes. *Calm down, damn it. Don't be a dweeb.* I pulled out the Luminol. My hands were shaking, damn them. The canister dropped to the floor with a clunk. Shit. *Okay, no one's here to hear the noise.* I picked it up thinking, maybe I should have read the directions beforehand. *Naw. Just look for any dark spots on the floor, shake the can and spray.* The blood would turn into a purple Van Gogh. I rolled the rug back, sprayed several spots and waited. Nothing. How long did it take? I sprayed again, held the flashlight up to the can and tried to read it. *Forget that; it should have lit up by now.*

Maybe Malik killed Christian in his own office or somewhere else—in the showroom next to one of those phony wooden elephants? I made for the door, hoping I had enough Luminol to check everywhere.

A bright flash made me jump. Overhead lights flicked on. I squinted and shielded my eyes. Two guys rushed me. *Shit-balls!* How had they gotten in without me hearing? Blue uniforms and badges. Police or security guards? The men pointed Glocks at me. *Goddamn. Better be cops.*

Chapter 22

JEFF

1995-96

At first Jeff imagined that, when he placed his hands on a sick man's forehead, it actually cured the fellow. Later he doubted. Soon, he understood. Still, there were some; the ones Bob Smithfield hadn't arranged, the ones who came with "miseries" and just needed a spiritual boost—Jeff did help people, at least those few. He did!

He and his mom traveled the south for months, guest preaching at different churches. Jeff's doubts grew. He lay awake nights, wondering, agonizing about the deceit. Fatigued, confused … discouraged. His mom brought him to their isolated place in New Mexico for rest. The stark beauty of the canyons, the silence, and the sunsets calmed him, but not enough. His dreams overflowed with grotesque people gawking at his hands, smirking, giggling behind his back.

"They think I'm a freak, don't they, mom?"

"No. No. No. No. They think you're wonderful."

"You told them I have the mark of God. You weren't supposed to say that."

"I didn't tell them your hands bleed. You insisted, and I didn't." Her tone was sharp.

"They still stare at them."

"I shouldn't have mentioned it. I'm sorry, but you *do* have the mark of God. You shouldn't be ashamed of it."

Jeff couldn't evade his doubts, his sleeplessness, the lingering exhaustion. One day his mom said, "I know what will cheer you up, son." She drove him to the animal shelter by the jail in Gallup, sixty miles from the cabin, where he picked out a beautiful brown and white collie. –Ruby.

After that, whenever his mom spoke harshly or shot him a condescending grimace, he reminded himself that she only wanted to make him worthy of God's gift. Her gift to him, Ruby, confirmed her deep, abiding love.

Ruby stayed in their motel rooms, as Jeff and Sarah performed at revival meetings from Texas to Florida, up to Nebraska and then retreated for rest at their isolated cabin. No television there, no internet, just the bible and other good books his mom selected. Jeff tried to study them, as she demanded, but he never escaped the exhaustion or the doubt. Sometimes, just sometimes, he was able to sleep with Ruby wrapped in his arms.

2000

THEIR FIFTH YEAR as itinerant preachers.

Jeff's mom was a celebrity, her pictures (and often their pictures together) on the covers of Christian magazines. He saw the way men looked at her after their performances, heard them compliment her, invite her out for a drink. Now a teenager, already seventeen, he recognized what they saw, an appealing blonde. Each man she rejected became a silent victory for Jeff, savored as he returned with his mom to their motel room to play board games, study, or watch TV.

The better he performed the holy-boy act, the more people worshipped him, the more his adrenaline pumped and his mother praised him. But also, the more melancholy he became when the crowds vanished and the thrill ebbed. Late at night, with his mom asleep in the other bed, Jeff felt exhausted but too jittery to sleep. He'd pull Ruby close absorbing her sweet collie warmth.

THE MORNING AFTER their second revival in Memphis, she waited outside their motel when Jeff took Ruby for her morning walk—a beautiful girl about his age, Jeff thought, wearing a pale blue dress. Modest-yet-enticing breasts, blond hair that shone in the sunlight. The dress clung to her buttocks just a bit. Her calves thrilled him. Normally he looked people straight in the eye, as mom had taught him, but this girl turned him shy. He gave her brilliant blue eyes a quick glance. He was so inexperienced! His mother had kept him that way, and he'd put up with it. There would be time to know girls, Mother said, to find a righteous woman, to marry. Until then, she told him, the only girl he should think of was her. He'd begun to realize; that was absurd. Weird.

He'd seen this girl a few times, he was sure—the most recent, last night at the revival meeting, looking up from the front of the crowd, her eyes shining. Her ADORATION fed him sunlight, fed him human warmth, passion—yes passion. So many in the congregation revered him, but this felt different. He'd wanted to step off the stage and talk to her, but there were two women in wheelchairs waiting to be *healed*. By the time he finished, she'd disappeared.

"Beautiful dog." She smiled shyly and gestured to Ruby.

He stepped closer, managing to look into her eyes. "I'm Jeff."

"I know. I saw you last night at the …" Her smile encouraged him. She walked to the end of the building and turned the corner.

He followed with Ruby trailing behind. "At the revival," he added. When he rounded the corner, he almost bumped into her. She beamed up at him. "You were … wonderful." She held her arms wide, and Jeff, without thinking, by God's natural enticement, pulled her close. She rose on her toes and kissed his cheek.

"I've seen you at five of the meetings." She kissed his neck. *Ohhh!*

Some people called them "groupies," the girls who followed a show, a musical act, a comedian, even a preacher. The way the light shone on her; she was pure and sweet and perfect. She might be an angel. Certainly not a *groupie.*

He kissed her ear. "I'm Jeff," he said again. She smelled like lilacs.

She laughed. "I've seen you heal people. You're amazing." She ran her fingers over his back. "Suzi, that's my name."

Jeff had never been in love. He'd never kissed a girl's ear or any part of one, never had his arms around one. His mother insisted on chastity. He felt guilty, as he kissed her cheek and moved toward her lips, just naturally about to—

"Easy, Jeff Lamb." She pulled back a few inches, smiling at him with what? —yearning—in her eyes. "I don't just go around hugging boys," she said. "But you're different. Tell me all about yourself."

Ruby wandered over by some bushes, as Jeff talked about his upbringing, his home schooling, Mom's religious ideas. Suzi told him about her favorite artists and musicians, her cocker spaniel,

Nellie, and her parents who argued all the time and ignored her. Still, they'd given her the greatest gift; a knowledge of Jesus Christ. After two years at a Christian college, she'd announced she wanted to follow her religious spirit. They'd bestowed their blessing and an American Express card with a $10,000 limit. Which meant that she was a little older than he was, but still innocent and perfect.

"Sad, isn't it?" she said. "They sent me away to school and now, all they want is to have me out of their hair." She smiled, but the smile was cheerless.

"Touch me, Jeff. Let me feel those healing hands, run them over my shoulders. I don't have pain, like those people you heal, but I have sorrow. I want to, I want to feel God's caress."

He would tell her he wasn't God. He didn't have healing powers, not really. But she was beautiful, and she seemed to idolize him. He wanted to keep touching, to explore. He stroked up her sides, feeling the ribs, her shoulder blades and slowly down to the small of her back.

"Thank you," she said, pulling back. "I feel *magnificent*." She closed her eyes, raised one shoulder and then the other, arching like a cat, her breasts under the blue fabric shifting, intoxicating him. "That feels sooo good, but ..." She opened her eyes wide. "Too good. I know you're holy, but I'm mortal flesh. I can't stay, you understand, because of the temptation."

"Wait." She was already walking away. He watched her lithe body—those shoulders, hips, buttocks, the little sad look she sent him, just before she jumped into a little red Chevy, waved and drove off.

In bed that night, he thought of Suzi, and he did something his mother would hate, and that she could never know.

SUZI CAME TO SEE the revival that next week in Chattanooga, there in the front row again, surrounded by zealous worshipers. He saw her ardent looks and watched helplessly, as she disappeared through the crowd after the last alleluia. The next morning at the motel, he went to get donuts for his mom, and found her, this time in a pale-yellow dress, beckoning him to follow.

Suzi took his hand and led him to a little stream behind the motel. "You healed those people. You have a gift." She kissed him, deep and thrilling.

Off to the left, he saw a path leading into the forest. "Let's go further back. I want to—"

"Jeff, no. We can't do that y-e-e-t-t-t."

She drew out the "yet," gazing into his eyes, wanting just what he wanted; he was sure. And what he would certainly not actually do.

"I only have a few minutes. Have to bring Mom her breakfast."

They hugged, and their hands ran over each other's backs. She patted his cheek and smiled into his eyes. "When I see you again, maybe we'll have more time." Her hand slid down his side, and he thought she would touch him in an intimate way, but she left again.

Twice more they met in two other cities, each time outside, alone, except for Ruby, but not private enough. Suzi said she adored him. She wanted him as much as he wanted her, but they agreed they couldn't sin. Each time she left him, she backed away, holding out her hand, as if she could lead him off to a love bed, but she forbid him to follow.

Until the next time, when they walked around behind another motel.

She reached for his hand—the left, the one that never hurt, but never quite healed—and stroked it. She tugged at his glove. "I want to see."

His gut turned over. "No. I can't." He pulled away.

"Please let me. Your hands are special. I want to be close to you."

One look at his repulsive left hand would send her running. "I want that too. I want to be intimate, Suzi. I love you."

"You will be, Jeff Lamb. You will be inside me. I will have you always." Her eyes shone with lust. "We'll have each other in ecstasy, immaculate and true."

"What?"

"You are divine, my love. Give me your light and your life, as God gave it to Mary."

No! She couldn't mean???

"I'm not God." –Beseeching.

"But you are. You heal people. I've seen it. You will have to go to heaven to rule, like in the bible. You'll leave me then, I know." Tears ran down her cheeks. "I must give you up, but I can keep you if we have a child. Give me what is pure and holy, and I will always be yours."

"You don't understand. I—"

"They will come for you," she said. "You know it. When the mob takes you; when they judge you and put you to death—" A tear ran down her cheek. "—I will carry your son. I'll hide and protect him, just like in the bible."

It hadn't occurred to him before, couldn't be true. Was Suzi crazy? Or some misguided groupie after all?

"No. I'm not. The cures; they're not all real."

She glowered at him, shaking her head. "That's a lie."

"I think I truly help some people. But the others, you must have seen. The man I pretended to heal in Chattanooga, the paralyzed one in the wheelchair, was the same one I *healed* in Memphis when he faked blindness."

Disappointment spread from her eyes and shattered her face. "I don't believe you."

"But this is real. I love you. When we hold each other, when I touch your hair, when you run your hands over my chest."

She glared at him. "You don't love me. Not at all. You don't want to give me a child to cherish. You could, if you wanted, just by wishing your seed into me." She looked at him hard for a minute and then hauled off and slapped him. It stung, and tears ran down his face. She stared, shocked. "Like Jesus," she said. "Christ on the cross. I've seen him cry in paintings." She ran fingers over his cheeks, dabbing the tears. She touched them to her eye lids. "Will this do it?" she asked. "Now I'll conceive?"

WHEN JEFF RETURNED with the bag of donuts, his mom flung it across the room. "I saw her." Her glare pierced him. "Your whore."

"She isn't Mom."

"A harlot, like in the bible, out to seduce you and steal your power."

He raised his left hand to silence her. "Suzi is pure, like—"

She grabbed the hand and squeezed hard. She let go, and he saw blood staining his glove. "Shame on you and on your bitch. When I find the right girl for you, I'll let you know."

Jeff had seen things on TV when his mother was out of the motel. He knew what other boys his age did with girls. Kissing and touching were the least of it. And Suzi had felt so very good.

That was the first time he hated his mom, but only for a day or two.

He never saw Suzi again, but in bed, in fantasies, in his dreams, he saw only her. This was his life, so sheltered by Mom with her home schooling and her overbearing rules.

And the deception! How could he have a life, let alone share a love, perpetuating those appalling lies?

CHAPTER 23

STAN

OCTOBER 28, SIX DAYS BEFORE ELECTION

Hannah left me a voicemail. "Come at midnight. Be quiet as a mouse. No need to disturb the neighbors."

That sounded sneaky but, more than that, intriguing!

I'd been thinking things over for the past couple of days. Hannah was separated!!! Her husband hadn't been good to her. She deserved someone who'd be kind. Was I the guy for that, or did I just want to relive that old fantasy? Show her what she'd been missing all these years? Solve the case to make her grateful?

Ecstasy for two! Or something more substantial?

She opened the front door, without turning on a light and without a mask. Once I got inside, she flicked on the lights. Beaming into my eyes, she said, "Glad to hear your Covid test was negative. Mine too."

She wore a silky dress, black with blue and green palms. It clung, showing off her great body. I pulled her close, and she pressed herself to me. We kissed like the high school lustful kids we'd been twenty-one years before. So perfect and so … wrong.

Married, and, yes, separated, her husband missing, and what was I doing? Swooping in to take advantage.

It looked like Hannah had made a decision about what she was willing to do with me—a delectable notion. If only I was more like Bud, more like a normal guy, or, on the other hand, more saintly. Either way would make this easier.

"We can't do this," I said. But my body, and my heart and my mind—no part of me—was willing to stop on its own. She pulled back just enough to run her hand down my chest.

"Don't worry, Stan. Jake and I don't really have a marriage anymore."

"You asked me to find him. You want to reconcile."

She responded with another hot kiss. Getting Covid tests had been a mistake. Coming here a mistake; I'd known that all day, even while imagining this moment. Adrenaline and testosterone were seducers, biological disasters. *Sure, blame it on them.*

My phone chirped. Bud calling. –Funny, he usually sent a text. I declined and silenced it.

"I need you here," she said. "You comfort me."

Sex, was that the comfort she needed?

"So, you want to *cuddle* again?"

She gave a wry smile. "Yeah, sure. Just touch me."

My fingers drifted down to that enticing derrière. If she'd wanted just cuddling, she would have worn something plush and loose. She would have worn a bra. If I wanted cuddling, I'd stop exploring. We kissed long and deep. She pulled back just a bit, smiled into my eyes as she gave a deep, satisfied sigh, and turned. "I can tell, you need a drink."

At the bar, she poured wine for herself, scotch and water for me. We each took a sip, and she handed me her glass.

Hannah picked up both bottles, scotch and wine. "This way to the pool." She led me through the open sliding glass door, set the bottles on a table, and grazed my cheek with her hand. "So amazing, our prom night."

"Oh, yeah."

"We could swim like that again."

She backed up a couple of steps and slipped the dress off, her body naked except for black undies. My eyes feasted. I set the glasses down, spilling half of her wine and a little scotch.

"I posed for you that night." She raised her arms over her head, showing off her chest.

I moved in, stroking the smooth curve of her tummy, my pulse running wild. "After that, we swam, but ..."

She turned into my arms, rose onto her toes, her body pressed against me, her eyes adoring. "You're still shy. I like that."

I slid one hand onto her breast, as the other stroked down her back.

"Better." She gave me a wicked smile. "We stopped a millimeter short of sex back then. We'll see tonight. Oh, Stan, this is so good, so much like old times."

She slipped out of my arms, dropped her undies to the ground, sprinted onto the diving board and sprang into the pool.

This was what I wanted, wasn't it? To consummate our prom night. Back then we'd refrained from that last act. Now we were adults; one single, the other almost. We could swim naked and then get dressed and just hold each other. We could.

Who was I kidding? I knew what I wanted; to dive into the pool, and then into Hannah. I pulled my shirt off and unbuckled my belt. Hannah surfaced by the side of the pool, her hair—almost black in the dim light—glossy, curling down past her chin. She gave me a little wave. "What are you waiting for, Stan?"

With my shirt off and pants about to fall, I thought my intentions were clear. I was unzipping my fly, when she said, "Don't feel guilty. My husband's dead, anyway."

Her words made my gut squirm and brought me back to Jake Christian. *Like a jackal, waiting for her husband to die.*

I stopped undressing.

She didn't seem to notice. "When you find Jake, if he's alive, he may be shacked up. You're my detective, Stan. I want you to report all the details."

Dead, she wanted him dead. If he was unfortunately alive, she needed dirt on him. Was she playing up to me because she liked me or for my so-called detective skills? Let her find someone else to fool with. I'd leave and finish the case as I'd promised, find out what happened to her husband. Jacob Christian … Married! … Indonesia … Luke! … Scarred hands … Bud's theories … Stigmata?

Something clicked then, from what Malik had told me, from Hannah too. Bud's various notions flitted in and out. "Hannah, you said Jake used to quote the bible?"

"Yeah, when we first met. He hadn't done it for years, until recently. So what?"

"Did he mention how he got the scars on his hands? Or talk about where he used to live? Maybe some particular religion?"

She snorted. "He never told me shit about his hands … He did mention Alaska, and one time he said something. Yeah, he said ministers are fake, but God is very, very real."

Interesting! "I have to use your computer. Do I need a password?"

She watched me, her arms resting on the side of the pool. My shirt was back on. I buckled my belt.

"I'm looking for your husband, remember? I might have a lead. This could be important."

"No password. Computer's on." She glared at me for a moment and then gave me the finger.

CHAPTER 24

I found Hannah's computer in the second room down the hall, jumped on and Googled *fake ministers*. Way too much information there. I tried *stigmata* just for Bud. Scads of information came up, including stuff about Saint Francis—not useful. Jacob Christian had appeared out of nowhere in 2001. Malik said he sold religion *to audiences*. There should be something on the internet.

I entered *missing preacher, 2001*, and a half dozen entries down, past the ads, I came to a piece titled, "Healing Preachers Disappear." From a Florida newspaper, it discussed a young man named Jeff Lamb and his mother, Sarah; an itinerant preaching team. Sarah and Jeff had drawn large crowds to revivals and church services throughout the south. In the second paragraph, I saw these eerie lines: "Miraculous healings abound …" and, "Jeff Lamb's healing hands, said to be the mark of God …" His hands!

I heard Hannah, in from the pool, stomping down the hall. Angry, abandoned not just by her husband but also by me.

It was hard to be sure from the black and white image of Jeff Lamb, but I thought I'd found Jake Christian! I felt a surge of adrenaline. Another piece from 1999 in Arkansas, showed a picture: Jeff Lamb and his mother, Sarah, wearing white robes with their gloved hands raised high. The caption: "On stage at Saturday's revival; the Dynamic Duo of Faith Healing." I was making progress!!!

"Hannah, come look." She walked into the room with a white towel wrapped around her body and another turbaned about her hair. She shot me a look and glanced at the computer. She moved in close.

"I'll be damned."

"Think this is him?"

"Move," she commanded. I jumped out of the way, and she settled at the computer, reading. "Wow. Is this what I married?"

"He told Malik he used to sell religion, and you told me—"

"You got a better picture?"

I leaned over her and took the mouse, feeling her head, in the damp towel, against my chest, so aware of her body close by. I paged back to the other article on the computer and stepped away. "These are the best so far. We'll find more tomorrow. In the meantime—"

"Okay, great, you've found something. *In the meantime, you can drag your ass out of here.*"

She looked pretty angry, so I headed for the door.

"Don't come back till you're ready for fun."

Later, back home, I ignored the red flashing light on the answering machine, shut down the ringer on my land line and went to bed. Hannah's body lingered in my vision. Hannah jumping into the pond twenty-one years ago, and again tonight. Hannah going off to college and cheating on me. So much pain back then.

I tried replacing Hannah's image with Melanie, another attractive woman, but what came up was, *I can't wait to tell Mel this news about Jake Christian.* I'd blown it with Hannah just like after high school, but what did I really want with her? Hannah was complicated; her moods erratic, not so different from my ex, Cheryl. If Bud were here, he'd say, "Fuck her, Stan and move on." Even the thought of him saying that annoyed me.

A sleeping pill later, I dozed off.

AT EIGHT THE NEXT MORNING, I called. Hannah's voice came on the answering machine and then a beep. "I'm sorry about last night, Hannah. It's just that … the idea of swimming with the wife of a guy who just died. Or, or who may not have died but needs help, a man in danger somewhere. I wouldn't feel right. Hannah, are you there?"

What I didn't say, *I dreamed of you so many nights after high school and again after we met at the reunion. Dreamed of meeting you in the moonlight, like last night. I'm so damned confused.*

"Hi, Stan." —Hannah's sarcastic voice. "You made me very sad last night."

"I apologize, but we need to sort this out about your husband."

"Yeah, fine. When *are* you going to sort this out?"

My screen lit up—a call from Mel. I declined it.

"We've got new leads, Hannah."

"Stan, darling, the sooner the better. You didn't like me saying Jake might be dead, but he could be."

"I can't think that way, Hannah."

"Your boy-fucking-scout idealism is wearing thin. Try thinking of Jake betraying his wedding vows with a hooker. Whatever he's doing I need to know. *Then* you can come frolic in my pool." —Sweet voice.

After I hung up, I imagined it for a moment, easy to picture after last night. My disappointed yearning kicked in, but also wariness. She'd gone from sarcastic to sweet in ten seconds. Bud's comments on the subject of Hannah popped into my head every time I thought about her now.

CHAPTER 25

October 29

I couldn't wait to tell Bud and Mel about Jeff Lamb. Bud would launch into conspiracy frenzy. Mel and I would make fun of him and laugh. Mel would find terrific new leads for us to follow. I called her.

"Stan, you've gotta—"

"Mel, wait till I tell you."

"Listen, Stan. The cops have Bud at the police station."

My chest went hollow. "I'm on my way, Mel."

After I hung up and jumped into the Escape, I thought about calling her back, asking more about Bud's situation. While I was at it, I could ask Mel to check out preachers named Sarah and Jeff Lamb. But Bud was in jail! Our cases didn't matter.

It wasn't hard to guess what Bud had done. He'd threatened to break into Malik's place, and he'd done it. This could really mess up Bud's life. And how about my business? Why hadn't I taken him seriously?

I waited two hours in a hard chair in the police station lobby. Behind a high counter, protected by plexiglass, a sergeant ignored me. It was warm. I took off my mask a couple of times to swipe the arm of my shirt across my forehead.

A plain clothes cop, about fifty, with greying hair, bushy eyebrows and a black mask emerged. He wore a white shirt, loose at the collar, and a green-and-yellow striped tie.

"I'm Waxman," he said. "Detective. You're here about Andrew Randolph?"

"Bud," I said reflexively.

He led me through a metal door and then stopped and backed me against the wall in the hallway. He was a few inches taller than me and hostile-looking.

"I'd charge him with breaking and entering, but he told me an interesting story. He says he's your partner. Says you're investigating a missing person's case."

Not Partners! Should I throw Bud under the bus or risk my business?

"A company called Sir Jacob Antiquities," the cop said.

"Oh, yeah. Absolutely. We questioned a guy named Malik there about a case."

Waxman gave me a hard look. "Your partner, this Andrew Randolph, says Malik's a suspect in the disappearance of a guy named Jacob Christian."

"You could say that."

He walked on ahead. Over his shoulder he said, "Come."

I figured this was all an act—a very good one—to intimidate me.

We entered a small, beige-walled meeting room. The first thing I noticed was Sirjay Malik sitting at the far end of a steel table. Malik wore a pale blue sport jacket and a canary yellow mask. He jumped to his feet as we came in. My stomach crawled around inside me.

There was one of those one-way mirrors on a side wall, and I wondered if anyone was watching.

"Sit." Waxman glared at Malik and pointed at a chair for me. We both followed orders. Waxman whipped off his mask and eyed me. "You think Jacob Christian is missing?"

"Right," I said.

"And *you* say he's in Indonesia."

Malik nodded. "Yes, detective, sir."

Waxman stood over me. "I met Christian's wife last week at her home. Beautiful place. Worried wife."

I looked down at the table, hoping the cop's breath didn't contain VIRUS. "Hannah … Mrs. Christian mentioned a police visit."

"I concluded that the husband took a break. Now you bust into Malik's offices trying to find a crime that didn't happen."

Bud, not me.

"Mrs. Christian asked us—"

Waxman tapped my shoulder, not hard, just firm. "Cops don't like people trying to show them up."

I made myself speak up. "We wouldn't do that."

"You and this Randolph guy have fucked things up. I phoned Mrs. Christian this morning to check your friend's story. Now she's yelling about how I'm not doing my job."

No wonder Waxman's tweaked.

"That's *one* of your problems," Waxman said. He thumped my shoulder again, a little harder. "Your other issue is this guy across the table. He wants us to lock you up for trespass."

Not me, Bud. Bud, my friend, my Army buddy, I had to get him out of this. If I were in jail, he'd find a way to help me. Bud wouldn't be submissive and weak. I couldn't be either. Nor could I charge in like he would.

"If Bud broke in," I said, "—and I don't know that he did—he was trying to do the right thing. He was looking for clues about Jacob Christian."

Waxman came around beside me, leaning close. "Do you have any evidence that this guy—" He jabbed a finger toward Malik. "—did anything to his partner?"

"Nothing direct, but—"

"'Nothing,' that's the word you just said. 'Nothing.'"

"We did find out that—"

"I don't give a rat's ass what else you got. Christian is taking time off from his missus. Period."

Malik cleared his throat. Waxman looked at him, and Malik spoke directly to me.

"You should not worry about Jake. I wrote an email to him and he wrote back only yesterday."

"You understand, dimwit," the detective said. "There is no case."

Malik gave the cop a quick glance. "Now Detective Waxman, there is to be charges for trespass, yes? Breaking and enter—"

I took a deep breath and charged in. "Mr. Malik, I'm sorry if Bud Randolph entered your store without permission. I have no knowledge of that. But it wouldn't be good for your business if the local news got wind of your partner's suspicious disappearance."

Waxman poked my shoulder and said, "You ain't going to do that."

I stared at Malik. "I don't want to."

Malik's look shifted from perturbed, to outraged, to thoughtful. "There's no reason for that to come out, sir. Not *disappeared*. Not *suspicious*. Not at all."

"It doesn't need to be a news item *or* a legal matter," I said. "If there's any damage, I'll pay for it."

"No. No. No damage. You wouldn't go to the newspapers, surely not."

"Okay, you two," Waxman said. "We ain't going to spend all day here. You, Stein, and you, Malik, will convince Hannah Christian that everything's okay. You, Malik, will forget about filing charges. Am I right?"

"Mrs. Christian won't listen to me," Malik said, and then he added, "There is also the matter of pretending to be—"

Waxman cut him off. "I'll take care of that. You can leave now, Mr. Malik, as long as you agree."

I wanted to head for the door with the merchant, but Waxman loomed over me. Malik turned back in the doorway, hitched his mask down beneath his chin and shouted at me, "Liar! You are not a police. Not a police." Then he hustled out.

"You owe me," Waxman said.

"Thank you."

"You seem like a reasonable guy, Stan Stein. I'm ordering you to control your idiot partner."

Not partner.

"I'll try."

"Make it work," Waxman said. "Impersonating a police officer can get you both locked away."

Bud, Bud, Bud.

"I actually didn't …"

Waxman looked like he was going to give me another tap, but he held off. "You were there that day. You were complicit, when your partner showed this guy the badge. I assume you've got some sort of investigator's license."

Damn it. One call from the police could close me down.

"So keep your mouth shut." Waxman gave me a chance to object, but I held my tongue. He lowered his voice. "If you don't act like an asshole, I'll release you *and* your partner. Stand up."

I stayed in my chair. "I'm going to be discrete about this."

Waxman pivoted around and gave me a look.

"I still have to investigate Jacob Christian's disappearance, to solve the case for his wife."

"Do what you gotta do, but don't rile that woman up. If I hear more about this, you're screwed." He led me into the hall. "Ditch your *junior G man* badge and make sure your partner does too. Now step in, and take a piss." He pointed to a men's room.

"Huh?"

"I'm going to keep your friend, Andrew, in his cell until I feel like letting him out. You could leave and let Andrew walk home, but that's not who you are. You'll be out in the waiting room for an hour, maybe three. Now take a piss and go wait."

Bud emerged four hours later. Outside, I said, "We wasted a day."

"Sorry." For once he looked repentant.

"You jeopardized my business."

He didn't say anything.

"You're not going to do this again, or we're both out of work."

After I dropped him off at his house, I started to feel good about myself. I'd backed Malik down and managed not to tick Waxman off. Yeah, pretty good.

Hannah didn't turn out to be as impressed, when I called. "Don't come tonight," she said. "Spend your damn time tracking down my cheating husband."

CHAPTER 26

JEFF

June 2001, Naomi, Nebraska

After Suzi, Jeff lost his remaining illusions about their *holy mission*. Pretending to be God frazzled the piss out of him. (Yes, defiant swearwords marched through his thoughts now and then.) How pathetic he felt, letting his mom control their lives. He was fucking 18 now. (That felt good!) A man but not manly.

He hadn't the heart to give another phony performance tonight, but he would, wouldn't he?

They stayed that afternoon in a dreary beige motel in rural Nebraska. Jeff craved sleep so bad, as he lay in bed, envying Ruby, who dozed beside him.

The door opened and his mom came in, carrying take-out bags. "Hamburgers and milkshakes, Jeff. Energy food. Time to eat and clean up."

Jeff sat up. Their two black suitcases lay open, on racks near the closet. Their white costumes hung in the doorless closet, taunting him with the message—*performance in two hours, you phony jerk.*

His mom sat down in the olive-green armchair, unwrapped a straw, thrust it through the lid of her milkshake and sucked.

Jeff walked over and took his burger. He settled back on the bed by Ruby, unwrapped his sandwich and took a bite, dreading tonight's charade. He stroked Ruby's sleek brown-and-white coat and ate a little more. He set the burger down in its wrapper and glanced at his mother, knowing her response before he spoke. "I can't stop worrying about our *act*." He said *act* harshly to make his point.

His mom set her drink on a table and gave him her *stupid boy* stare. "It'll be easy, son. Like all the others."

He glowered at her. "You know what I'm talking about, Mother, *the lies*."

She stood, holding her milkshake. "Not that again."

"It's just that—"

"We're engaged on the noblest *act* in all humanity." She moved in and hovered over him. "We promote the Lord's good works. He heals people. He does. You heal people too, *a few*. I was hoping you'd be better at it." She took a slow sip of her milkshake, watching him. "You disappoint me, son. If you had more faith, you would heal more and question less."

Almost all of the ones I heal are fake, he thought. But maybe she was right. Once in a while, one of the people he touched—a person who showed up that night out of the blue, complaining of deep despair—seemed truly relieved by Jeff's touch.

There was no point in discussing this; he knew the outcome. The next question, he'd raised only once before, but it ruined his sleep lots of nights: "You claim we're raising the money to do good works." *But you hide it under the floorboards and lodge it in foreign banks.*

His mother hadn't answered him that previous time, but now she laser-ed him with cool confidence. "I have such plans for that money, Jeff. Next year, we'll tour Europe to spread the holy message. That will cost a great deal." A dreamy smile spread over her face. "Then on to India. We'll open a center there to praise good works. We can call it *Healing Heart*, better yet, *Jeff's Healing Hands*. What do you think?"

He wanted to believe that would be a good purpose. But to accept that, he'd have to trust their mission. His mother was the mission, and deceit was the method, but his heart could not let him disappoint her tonight, especially with so many people coming to see them. His mother returned to her chair and took a triumphant sip from her milkshake.

"Here girl." Jeff took the rest of the meat from his bun and held it out. Ruby wolfed it down happily.

Couldn't his mom comprehend how wrong this was? Hadn't she seen his energy deplete with every new crowd in every new city, with every fake healing? He'd made it through the last few Sundays, just barely, but this couldn't go on.

THAT WAS THE NIGHT Jeff collapsed onstage. When he came to, he heard mumbling from scores of people milling around in the tent. He felt something touch his arm. He opened his eyes to find a paramedic checking his pulse.

The next day Sarah Lamb and her son retreated with their collie, heading for their cabin in Navajo country. Jeff sat in the back seat with Ruby, her head protruding through the open window. His hand was on her side, his mind far away.

This malaise wasn't just about lack of sleep, or about the charade they played onstage. His physical collapse was minor compared to his collapse of faith in her. What she'd done to all the people, stealing their souls, she'd done to Jeff ten times over. By the time they reached the cabin, he couldn't look at his mother. Ruby was the only honorable creature in that car.

Two weeks later, lacking the courage to face his mom, Jeff took off. He abandoned faithful Ruby, took his mother's money and her car and ran.

CHAPTER 27

JUNE 2001 - 2002 NEW MEXICO TO SANTA MONICA CA

When Jeff, at eighteen, escaped the cabin in New Mexico, he spent six months in Alaska, dying his hair, growing a beard, changing his identity. He obtained a driver's license that made him four years older, enough time to have earned a phony college degree. He chose the name Jacob, the biblical younger son who usurped his brother's birthright. Last name, Christian. –Right.

He moved to LA. With his mother's money, he rented a place in Santa Monica a few blocks from the boardwalk. With no sense of purpose, no sense in general, he wandered. His money was depleting. Hopeless, useless, no longer a celebrity, he needed a direction. One day he came across a poster for a motivational talk: *Make your Fortune. Make your Life*. Jeff attended and spoke up a few times in the first session.

At a break between meetings, he stood alone, questioning why he'd come. An Indian man approached. He handed Jeff a plate with a muffin on it. "My name is Sirjay Malik. Is this what you seek?"

Jeff laughed. "The conference isn't about pastries. It's about making my life work."

"I could tell from what you said in the meeting; you're hungry for something. This muffin is but a token."

Jeff took a bite and realized he *had* been hungry. He remembered a bible verse and quoted it for the man. "It will be as when a hungry man dreams, and behold, he is eating. But when he awakens, his hunger is not satisfied."

Malik asked him if he'd thought of working in sales.

"Sure," Jeff said. "And I have loads of experience."

Malik chuckled. "You're so young. How much could you have?"

"More than you imagine, Mr. Malik. I'm twenty-two, and I've convinced audiences all over the south to buy my pitch."

"What pitch was that?"

"Religion, Mr. Malik and ..." *and bullshit.* "I sold healing words from the scriptures."

Malik looked him over. "You're a handsome young man. You speak well. If you can sell religion, surely you can peddle statues."

AFTER AN HOUR conversing in the hotel coffee shop, Malik offered a job, and Jeff accepted. The first day at the antique store, the merchant insisted on seeing Jeff's hands. His mouth twisted in revulsion.

"You shine with the innocence of a dove. You speak with the enticement of a siren. But you won't succeed with those ... objectionable scars."

Malik tracked down a cheap plastic surgeon and paid part of the cost. Jeff's hands were repaired. He sold more artwork in two weeks than Malik had the previous month. His confidence soared.

One customer, a beautiful brunette named Hannah, returned a second time, and a third. Jeff invited her for coffee. They spent three hours at coffee shop, as Hannah laid out her sorrows over a recent breakup.

Maybe she was as lost as Jeff. Maybe he baffled her with the stories he made up about his life. Within a week, they were holding each other on her sofa, sharing (fake) confidences. Within two, she took him into her bed. Making love with Hannah was more transformative than anything he and his mother had offered in their *healing* sermons. They married three months after that long afternoon at the coffee shop.

Needy, innocent beyond belief, his spirit destroyed by his mom, his soul reeling; he'd anchored to a seductive unsubstantial island. It was funny or maybe tragic. In life nothing made a damned bit of sense.

CHAPTER 28

STAN

OCTOBER 30, ELECTION 4 DAYS AWAY

It wasn't Bud's fault. I kept telling myself that. It wasn't even Trump's fault, not completely. The spiritual crisis in America had been brewing for years. Trump exposed and exploited it, picking at a scab that should have been left in place. Still, every time I looked at Bud, I couldn't help seeing the smarmy smirk of that evil man. *Evil*—had I ever described a living person that way? But here it was, and here was my friend, his admirer. I took a Xanax, stressed about my next encounter with Bud and feeling disheartened at America's broken soul.

The morning after the encounter with Detective Waxman, I picked up Starbucks cappuccinos for Mel and me and brought them to the office. She wore a blue plaid shirt and tan jeans, no mask and no glasses. I gave her the drink and backed up just far enough. *You're pretty Mel, I'm noticing more and more.* —I didn't say that. We looked at each other for a minute. Then I told her about Googling *missing preacher* and finding Jeff Lamb.

"Wow," she said. "Let me check this out." She started working on her computer.

While she dug into Jeff Lamb, I headed out to keep an eye on one of our potential workers' comp scammers.

I was sitting in the Escape in a middle-class suburban neighborhood, one of those places with mid-twentieth century, cookie-cutter houses and matching trees on both sides of the street, when she called.

"Stan, that was fantastic, the way you found Sarah and Jeff Lamb. They starred at revivals in the Dakotas, Arizona and the deep south. For years, they filled mega-churches in Florida and Georgia for guest appearances. Twenty years back they disappeared."

"AWOL, right?"

"Yup. Starting in '01. But the mother showed up in Florida a few months ago, preaching Sundays at the Lord's Chapel near Miami."

Through the windshield, I noticed a young woman ride by on a bicycle; the third time she'd passed. She gave my car a good look, as she rolled by. I figured she was memorizing my license plate. She'd call the cops if I didn't move on.

"That's a great lead," I said. "See what else you can dig up on her role in that church."

"Here's a fun fact," Mel said. "Back in the nineties, they performed lots of healings. Jeff laid his hands on people in wheelchairs. They jumped up and danced for joy. And they had another gimmick."

I waited, but she didn't elaborate, wanting me to ask. "Which was?"

"Jeff and his mother always wore white gloves, and she insisted he'd been touched by God. People claimed his hands bore some holy mark."

Just like Bud said. "You don't believe in that, do you, Mel?"

"Not for a minute."

The sweet sound of Mel's satisfaction was music to my ears. We'd been laughing together more lately. I wanted to be closer, to hear more of that. But I had to move the Escape. "Mel, before I hang up, I want to ask you." I took a breath and said, "Would you consider going out with me?"

"A date?"

"Something like that. Maybe it's a bad idea. If you don't want to—"

"Absolutely yes, Stan."

"How about Sunday?"

"Great."

I felt a happy rush. "Super." Mel wasn't as hot as Hannah—*showy*, that was the word—or as eager for my body. But Mel was pretty. She was nice, smart, unmarried, uncomplicated, or so I imagined. *Trustworthy.*

I thought about Mel a lot that night, and Hannah—whose angry flare-ups upset me—not as much as before. I considered our case too. I couldn't trust Bud to stay on track, so I'd be the one to travel to Florida and interview Sarah Lamb. What did it take to go onstage and lay *healing hands* on people? Was Jeff Lamb really Jake Christian, his twin, or … Was he a cynical charlatan or crazy as hell? Bud's voice insinuated itself into my reverie: *What if the sucker is fuckin' Jesus, come to haunt us?* And another of Bud's phrases, *This is sure fun.*

CHAPTER 29

SATURDAY OCTOBER 31

B ud and I were out for a rare Saturday surveillance. I drove the
Escape, with him in back, through a residential neighborhood.
Red-white-and-blue Trump banners hung from flag poles at two
adjacent homes.

"Good Americans," Bud said.

I left that one alone.

"I guess you're not worried about the election," he said.

"I'm damned worried."

He rat-a-tatted the back of my seat with both hands, like a
drummer. "The steal, that's what eats me."

I'd seen Trump on the news a few times, saying that he could
only lose if the election was a sham. My stomach slid up into my
esophagus. It felt wrong being confined with Bud in this vehicle.
Not only because of his bare face or the way his break-in had
jeopardized my business. Trump's treasonous pronouncements
were the biggest factor.

What was a guy to do if he had to say something, but he
knew it would turn into a sack of putrid slime the minute he
spoke up?

"I have to say it, Bud." I looked in the mirror and saw him watching, ready to pounce on whatever I said. "I told you four years ago that Trump was the Manchurian Candidate, right? Now it's obvious."

Bud scoffed. "Just because he has a bromance with Putin …"

When a man has a good friend, when something really bothers him; they should be able to talk it out. That's what I'd always thought. Truth and reason should matter. "Four years ago, Trump thought he'd lose, so he made a big deal about how the election was rigged."

"Well, yeah."

"And well, yeah, he won. So, it wasn't rigged. Now, he's losing, so he's selling that garbage again. He won't even commit to leave office when he gets trounced. He's not an American, not at all."

"It *is* rigged," Bud said, visibly warming up. "Everyone knows that."

His enthusiasm was my regret, but how could I stop now? "All those dead people voting. Yeah."

"You got it."

"If I was dead, I'd vote for Trump, just to spite everyone who outlived me." –Not funny. A damned mistake. I should have made my real points: Trump had no evidence that lots of people would cheat. If he did, he'd reveal it. More likely, he realized that all those absentee ballots this year would do him in.

Too late to say any of that, now that Bud was getting fired up.

"Trump knows what's going on. He's the leader of the free world."

"No. That's a nice woman in Germany, named Angela who has a conscience." Damn me for getting drawn in.

Bud leaned forward and rested his arms over the back of the passenger seat. "I thought you were a better American."

As usual, the argument was veering off course, but how could I refrain? "Trump might as well be working for Putin, the way he denigrates our elections—and our country, by the way."

"You give me a guy named Boris, and I'll raise you the Deep State."

How could Bud—how could anyone—not see through Trump's phony rubbish? How could he not take this seriously? Every cell in my body wanted to speak truth to nonsense. But the two of us had been over this so many times. My blood pressure demanded an end.

"I'll tell you this," Bud said. "America has been giving up to the competition. We can't even build a damned washing machine anymore."

Bud actually had a point there, but this whole discussion hurt my soul.

"Okay, enough."

It was lunchtime, but I wasn't hungry. Bud would be; nothing ever curbed his appetite. I spotted a Burger King and pulled to the curb out front.

"You started it," Bud said.

I hadn't started it, but I wouldn't contribute further.

"You questioned Trump's patriotism." He cracked the back door open. "You're kicking me out, right?"

"Yeah." I nodded toward the hamburger place. "Get your lunch. I'll pick you up after."

My cell rang. It was Melanie. Apparently she was working Saturday too. I hit *Answer* on the dashboard.

Mel sounded excited: "You know how I told you that Sarah Lamb began preaching in Florida. Turns out she's telling her parishioners to ignore Covid and attend church. No masks. Lots of gospel singing."

"Good plan," Bud said. "Except for the church bit."

"Here's the most fascinating part," Mel said. "Sarah Lamb went missing and didn't preach the last two Sundays. No one knows where she went."

"Hot shit," Bud said.

"I have more. Sarah Lamb voted in McKinley County, New Mexico back in 2000."

"Super job, Mel," I said.

"Okay, you guys, that's all I've got. Going to cook lunch for my mom now." Mel hung up.

"*Fucking amazing,*" Bud said. "I thought Jake Christian had gone to see mommy dearest in Florida. Now she's evaporated too. Stan, this changes everything."

"Sure, Bud. Have a nice lunch."

Sitting alone in a nearby park, I pondered, the soul-wounding nature of our conversations about Trump. Not a good-natured contest between political rivals—was that something that really happened in the past? Now, in 2020, we were discussing a man doing everything he could to discredit American democracy. Not a rivalry but a tragedy, because both sides believed the other candidate would destroy our country.

I picked Bud up after lunch and drove toward his apartment. "Let's take a few days, pal, maybe a week, off."

"Yeah?"

"This election stuff is intense."

I glanced in the mirror and saw Bud, narrow-eyed.

"We breaking up, partner?" His voice choked up.

"I need a breather. I'll send you an email if we get new cases for you."

"Huh?" He paused and then began singing the old song: "They say that breaking up is ha-ard to do-oo. Now I know. I know that it's true-oo ..."

"You all right with that?" I pulled to a stop in front of his apartment building.

"Sure partner, but let me give you some advice."

"What about?"

"Break it up—you and Hannah."

"I made her mad and haven't seen her in a couple of days."

"I get it, partner," he said. "I'm a red-blooded guy. Hannah's bod tickles your gonads. She gives you moony eyes and tells you how goddamned handsome you are. She's one beguiling piece of ass."

"You *don't* get it, Bud. She and I have a history."

"That's just some figment of your testosterone-soaked fantasies. I'm telling you, Stan, don't trust that woman." He opened the car door but didn't get out. "Or, the other option; fuck her brains out."

"Bud!"

"Test your theory, man. If you think she likes you, see if she'll go all the way."

"Life's more complicated than that."

"Says the guy who only believes stuff he hears on CNN." Bud got out, and I sat with the engine idling. It was easy to dismiss his political nonsense; not so much his thoughts about Hannah.

Chapter 30

BUD

November *1, 2*

Stan, my best friend, had banished me from work. Fine. Good. Trump would win the election, no problem. Stan's feelings would be hurt. Boo-hoo. I'd taunt him about losing. How could I resist? Stan would hate the piss out of it and then forgive and forget. That was Stan. I loved and protected him. We'd faced death together in the Army. Pals. But these days Stan acted superior. *Conspiracy theories;* that was a cheap expression to down my ideas.

Hannah had fucked me over by firing my ass. Neither of them gave a crap for my opinions. I'd solve the Christian case and show them. Piece of cake.

It came down to a simple equation: Jake Christian was Jeff Lamb was Sarah Lamb's son. Both had gone missing, had lived in New Mexico. A few days without Stan's interference—perfect. Let him fiddle with workers' comp diddly-shit. I would carry the only real case we'd had this year, force them to admit my genius.

New Mexico or Florida? –An easy choice: heading east from LA in my Mustang, I'd hit New Mexico first. If that lead turned sour, I'd keep on going. I drove to Hannah Christian's neighborhood and parked a few houses down, in front of Abel Ramirez's house. I'd recruited Ramirez by knocking on doors a few days back. Simple detective work.

I rang the doorbell, and Abel answered. He was a handsome Latino, mid height, wearing one of those yellow alligator shirts. We shook hands, and I passed him the envelope.

"Hey Abel. I really appreciate your help with my case."

"No problem. Easiest hundred I ever made."

"Let me in, and I'll grab my equipment."

"Sure." Abel headed inside. A minute later his garage door rolled up. Abel watched as I boxed the receiver and tablet computer.

"You mind telling me who you were recording? Someone on my block?"

"Sorry." I couldn't help smiling, as I said, "We detectives like to keep things on the down low."

Back at my apartment, I listened to Hannah's phone conversations from the past few days. So that was what the bitch had in mind. It would piss Stan off, but he needed to hear this. I copied a few of the conversations between Hannah and her lawyer on a flash drive, and then took a sleeping pill and fell off for several hours.

At 5:00 AM, I dropped a note for Stan with the recording at the office and headed east. By 7:00 AM I was doing seventy-five on I-40, off to New Mexico.

CHAPTER 31

JEFF

December 2017

Sixteen Years After Jeff Fled the Cabin

Everyone called him *Jake* these days, but he could only be *Jeff* in his head (not that he wanted to be). When he'd first been married; as he worked with Malik to advance and become a partner in Sir Jacob Antiquities; as he'd become the parent of a baby, who became a toddler, a youth, a fifteen-year-old; Jeff had toiled without rest. So full of activities and duties, he had no time to dwell on his earlier life as a holy fraud.

Now his son was a teenager, and Jeff barely saw him. His wife insulted him. His partner belittled him. Idle for long hours, drinking his gin, he contemplated. His past crowded out his now. Images flooded his dreams: Jeff sporting his white suit, his mother in her robe, preaching to hundreds, ashamed of every word of their unholy act.

He couldn't reveal his shame to Hannah or Luke. Couldn't even tell his shrink, Dr. Newhart. Nonetheless, the psychiatrist knew enough to advise, "You must go back to the origin of your pain and beyond it. Find a place and a time when you encountered contentment. Regain that feeling and make it part of you again."

The cabin! Back when his father had been alive, they'd wandered among the gullies and atop the mesas. They'd driven to Colorado and examined the tailings from abandoned mines around Silverton. His dad shared his reverence for the land and for nature, shared his dreams of making their fortune in veins of gold. Much later, the cabin had been a retreat for Jeff, his mom, and Ruby, bringing him what little peace he knew in their preaching days.

Outside Crownpoint, New Mexico

IT WAS A SHORT WALK from where Jeff parked the Bronco, the path he'd taken often all those years ago. He'd been in her spell then. *Bitch or saint? Enemy or beloved?* What if he found her—if she was even alive?

"Our secret place," she used to call it. "Our refuge of peace. Holy shrine."

On a gentle night that first time with just her—he'd probably been ten—they lay on blankets, gazing at the night sky, the majesty of God's creation, ethereal, immense.

She hummed Amazing Grace and asked, "Who loves you the most in all the world?"

"You, Mom."

"In all the universe?"

"You, you, you."

"And who do *you* love the most?"

He'd nuzzled his face against her arm and answered, "I love you, Momma."

She'd hummed another hymn as he fell off to sleep.

Not all had been holy or serene. Jeff discovered that. She had a bank account in the Bahamas, another in Switzerland, thousands in hundred-dollar bills under the floorboards. They'd come often to this place where God felt close. *God's son,* she called Jeff. *Holy Jeffrey.* What a crock of shit.

The cabin lay sixty miles from Gallup, at the edge of Navajo country. Native people, *Diné,* believed their ancestors ascended from within the earth. Still his deeply Christian mother said the Navajo were blessed by Jesus. Jeff reached the crest now and spotted the cabin. He stopped cold. The same, but unfamiliar. Small, plain. Feelings coursed through him: fear, loathing, warmth, devotion; currents that had simmered inside him, demanding to boil out, as his marriage and his life deteriorated.

He'd loved his mother so much.

She ruined him, she hurt him.

She made him what he was. Which was what? Charming, clever … a soulless pile of shit.

The shrink said he had a *Mother Wound.* Right. He said that once Jeff faced his *Mother Wound,* he *might* be able to heal his marriage. What did he know?

He pictured his mom, in her white gown, presenting Jeff onstage. He made a show of raising his hands and making them tremble, the white gloves shimmering in the spotlight's glare. Then he would descend to the front of the audience where he would "heal the infirm."

Sometimes, after a few drinks, he found this image hilarious. Laughed like a mad man. No, no, no. Not mad. Not mad, and not today. Mother disappeared from public view sixteen years ago, just after Jeff left. No one on this earth could say where to find her.

Except possibly him.

He had to find out.

He didn't want to know.

Moving closer, seeing the weathered boards, shutters closed over the windows, old, bare wood turning almost gray. The roof over the little square porch, askew. Floorboards squeaked as he stepped up. He laid his palm against the doorframe. He could hear her voice. "I love you so, Jeff. I couldn't live without you." He'd threatened to leave a few times, but those words had always stopped him … until they didn't.

What if he found her shriveled corpse?

He broke free all those years ago. The shrink said to give himself credit.

She ruined me.

She made me a star. She raised me up. She tore me down. I want to kill her.

I long for her to hold me.

No sound but the wind. *Leave and never come back.* He knocked, knocked again. He tried the knob, feeling the twinge in the palm of his hand—exquisite pain—as he grasped it harder. Could he still make it bleed if he squeezed really hard?

He found the key beneath that rock by the pinion pine, inserted it, jiggled. He could break a window if he needed to. He rattled the door, pulled it to him. The key turned. Door creaked on its hinges.

Don't go in.

He entered. Musty. Jeff managed to open the front window and released the shutters for light. Same picture of Jesus preaching the sermon on the mount. The Lord was watching him from that shelf, His eyes following, His head turning to observe (and judge), as Jeff moved around the cabin. Imagination or hallucination? He looked over, and Jesus winked at him. That might have surprised him once, but not the way he'd been lately.

Not just mold; the odor a little sickening. He pried open the old latches on the windows by the kitchen sink. The one beside the refrigerator fell off in his hand—termites. A chilly breeze rewarded him. No body … yet. A dusty picture lay on the desk: the two of them, in white outfits, looking ecstatic. There'd been hundreds like this, autographed for the masses. He turned it over and found a note in her precise handwriting:

September 5, 2001

> *Jeff, I am despondent. I've waited so long for your return, two months now. I've fed your dog and walked her, but she's your dog. I have no need of her. You might think I'd be angry that you took all of that money and ran—$50,000 wasn't it? —our truck too. I'm not, Jeff. The problem is that you cannot forsake our mission. You'll come looking for me one day, but, like you, I've fled. The heathens of America turn their backs on God. I'm called to Indonesia where simple people still hear with open ears and see with clear eyes. When you're ready to resume our blessed journey, God will lead you to me. And Jeff, I hope you come back soon. Ruby depends on you.*
>
> *Love U*
> *Momma*

Jeff took in a long slow breath, relieved. The smell in the cabin was just old mold, not his mother's rotting corpse. At the door to his old bedroom, the odor stronger, his heart beat hard.

Don't be a goddamned wimp.

He opened it. The air more sour still. Jeff glanced around the bedroom and yanked the bathroom door open; air so heavy he sipped it through his nose. There in the corner, lay the body—tufts of fur, white and fawn-brown. A bone protruded. He poked it with the toe of his shoe. Part of a leg? He pushed aside some fir—ribs, black flaky parchment—skin, a hole where the eye had been. Ruby, her remains preserved by the dry climate. His beautiful collie. He'd been desperate to cut and run back then. He'd *slept* outside the cabin that night, while Ruby and his mother stayed inside. Couldn't afford to have Ruby barking to wake his mother. Jeff slipped away in the night like a traitor.

Had she poisoned Ruby? He saw scratch marks on the back of the bathroom door. Black slashes—blood. She'd been locked in here to starve. He could hear her desperate barking, see her clawing, paws bloody. He felt her resignation, as she curled up by the sink to wait for Jeff, who wouldn't return for 16 years. The stare of her missing eye now condemning him. That's what the note meant. Tears streamed down. He'd all but forgotten Ruby. Now he wanted to scoop her up and cradle what was left in his arms. He ran outside and puked beside the front porch.

THE CABIN SAT on a forty-acre plot in the *checkerboard area,* where Navajo land met small parcels of private property. Jeff's mother got along with her Navajo neighbors. They seldom spoke, but when they did, she asked about their spiritual beliefs. The closest Native-American family, named Begay, grazed their sheep unencumbered here. Jeff's mother received occasional offerings of sheep's milk or cheese. The Begays would not have thought of disturbing the cabin, even when abandoned all these years.

The Navajo presence sanctified this land, a fitting place to bury his dog. Jeff found blankets in the closet and a shovel in the shed behind the house. He scraped Ruby's remains onto a blanket and wrapped her—so light when he lifted the bundle. He set her on the ground near the edge of the mesa. Taking a deep breath, he scanned the horizon. There, off to the north, the view he remembered. On these clear winter days, if smoke from the Farmington power plant wasn't hanging heavy across the horizon, little white pyramids shone, the San Juan Mountains of Colorado, a hundred miles away.

He buried his dog in that peaceful place.

CHAPTER 32

2018-2019, Santa Monica CA, Indonesia

Jeff's marriage was shakier than ever, but he had to keep trying. His son had turned on him—teenagers! Americans were at war with each other over religion and common decency, white supremacists coming out of the woodwork.

And his nightmares! What a mistake it had been to visit the cabin last year! The vision of Ruby's carcass came often. The eyehole in her parchment skin stared at Jeff in his sleep. His mother came in the night too, preaching holy bullshit, sometimes to a congregation of farm animals. Jeff needed to find her, to denounce her for so many things. Did he think his 'momma' would absolve him of his sins, past and present? Turn him into a decent man, decent husband? Send him on a U-turn on the road to sanity? He followed his mother's note to Indonesia, a sprawling country made up of islands. Muslims dominated most of them, but there were Christian pockets here and there.

He inquired at the most prominent Christian churches in Jakarta without success. On business trips the next year, he island hopped from Jakarta to Christian cities on other islands, seeking Sarah Lamb at every church. With thousands of islands, any one could have concealed his mother. They concealed her well.

At the end of his last trip, resting on a lounge chair by the sea in Bali, a waiter brought his third Bintang beer. The waiter, wearing a loose-fitting shirt covered with images of tropical foliage, moved on to another table, where two older couples waited to place their orders.

Jeff drank. The palm trees rustled. Hazy mountains beckoned from across the sea. The gentle lapping of water made him sleepy.

> *Jeff is seventeen, dressed like Elvis in a white sequined jumpsuit, onstage before thousands, Easter Sunday. He raises his hands, which are pure white alabaster, sparkling in the sun. People gasp and shout. "Jeff Lamb, we love you. Bless us Father Jeff. Pastor Jeff, grant us peace. Lord Jeff, bring us to your Eternal Home." Jeff knows, even in dreamland; he isn't Father Jeff or Pastor Jeff. He isn't Lord or eternal. He is truly the most unworthy boy on earth. Still, he's euphoric. He's fooling them all. They worship him! An electric guitar appears, strapped across his chest. "Pastor Jeff, sing us Are you Lonesome Tonight."*

He'd had dreams like this before, but when he came out of this one, he was standing, his arms outstretched like a performer. *What the fuck?*

The four tourists gawked at him. Ruby sat on the sand by his feet—the Ruby of his memory, a perfect, healthy collie.

No, no, no, no. Ruby couldn't be there. He was still dreaming, obviously, but this was so real.

"Was I singing?" he asked the dog.

Ruby gazed up at him. *You're wasting your talent on these* schmucks, she said without opening her mouth. *Come home to the mesa and sing for me.* —The collie's voice like a sweet young woman's.

He headed back to his room at the hotel, feeling the sand between his toes and the breeze on his cheeks. He was awake and yet he'd been conversing with one seriously dead canine.

Not Lord Jeff—psycho Jeff.

CHAPTER 33

STAN

NOVEMBER 1

I arrived at Arrucci's Restaurant in Manhattan Beach at two. There were chairs set under an arbor by the entryway, and Melanie rose from one of them. She wore a light blue dress and one ruby stud in her left earlobe. Smiling shyly, she stood taller than me by at least an inch. I looked down, and saw not only silver, sparkly high heels but her shapely brown calves. *You look really good in that dress!* My eyes moved up slowly. *Very shapely.* I avoided scanning back down and looked into her eyes. She had a black mask on, but I thought about saying, *Mel, the top third of your face looks great with makeup,* and asking, *Why only one earring?* I didn't. I let my admiring gaze meet hers and gave her a not-too-quick embrace.

"Nice hug," she said.

The host brought menus and showed us one of the outdoor tables, spaced out beneath red and green umbrellas.

We ate an antipasto and veal. We drank martinis, laughing about Bud and his theories. I pointed out that she'd had a few of her own. We spoke quietly about the election, lest we be overheard. Trumpers were everywhere, even here in California. Some would love to argue his virtues.

"Want some wine or another martini?" I asked.

We agreed on a bottle of Chianti. "I'm not a good date," I said. "Not able to drive you home after this wine."

"No problem. I took a cab here. I'll catch another back."

"You don't like Uber?" I asked.

"Don't like putting cab drivers out of work."

Good for you, Mel, I thought.

Wondering about Mel, a 35-year-old woman, living with her mom. "I shouldn't pry, but I've been curious… you and your mom …"

She waved that away with a subtle flick of her hand. "That's okay. She's not well. Emphysema, a bad case."

"You've got to *really* worry about Covid."

"My sister and I are keeping her safe. Where I live with mom, it's the house where I grew up. She's rooted there, so we're making improvements. My brother-in-law gave it a new paint job and we had AC installed."

We watched as a waiter opened the wine and offered me the cork. I declined the honor. He poured two glasses. When he was gone, I asked, "Think you'll ever move?"

"I had an apartment for years, but I came back to help Mom. It would be hard to leave her."

We were quiet for a minute, and I said, "I'm glad you didn't wear your glasses again today, and I love that dress."

She gave me a look, like she was deciding what to say.

"Sorry I'm your boss, sort of. Maybe I shouldn't mention personal stuff."

"Boss or not, I'll slap you down if I need to." She said it with a smile that made us both chuckle.

"You're a straight arrow, aren't you, Stan?" I must have looked hurt, because she added, "I like that about you. I like it a lot. Too many crooked arrows in my life." She swirled the wine in her glass and sipped.

"Black guys?" I regretted the question the second it was out.

She gave me a quick, harsh glance, then stared at the table. "Black, Anglo, Latino; snakes slither in every field, and if you don't know that—"

"I shouldn't have said it. Total mistake." I held my hands up in surrender and waited a moment until she looked at me again. "You left out Chinese and Native American … Vietnamese; all reptiles, no doubt."

She looked almost amused, but still not quite happy.

"I hope you won't give up on me over one dumb comment."

She took a breath, shook her head and said, "I've been thinking that you're one of the good ones, Stan. Don't disabuse me of that happy illusion." She looked straight at me like she was trying to decide to be angry or not.

"I'll try to avoid it. You were telling me about your mom."

"—She lives downstairs and I'm up top. Our garage is full of oxygen tanks and inhalers. My sister's down the block with her husband and little girl. She and I are the two musketeers; one's always on duty." She looked up at the sky, twisted her head right and left, like she was trying to get the kinks out. She had a pretty neck.

"Sorry you have that responsibility."

"You apologize too much, Stan. Do you know that? Bud walks up and down your face. You say, 'Forgive me, Bud. I hope my nose didn't get in your way.' You turn someone in for workers' comp fraud, and you feel crappy for hours. You want to apologize to me now; I know you do."

"You must think I'm a sap. But you'll be happy to know, I told Bud to stay away until after the election."

Mel gave me a quizzical look and reached across the table. She laid her hand on mine. Her fingers were long and warm. I'd been enthralled with Hannah these last few days, pale olive complexion and hazel eyes. Now I was starting to think that chocolate was an excellent color for a woman's skin.

"As I said, I like the way you are." She looked down at our hands. "We'll have to use sanitizer eventually, but I'm in no hurry to let you go."

I wasn't either.

Chapter 34

November 1, 2

That night, after my date with Melanie, I needed a late snack. I microwaved a Costco grilled chicken sandwich a little too long, but there was no odor. I supplemented the chicken with tomato, onion, and mustard. It tasted really bland. I doubled up on the mustard. No help. In the bathroom, I found the after shave I hadn't worn since Cheryl. No smell. Rats!

Monday morning, I woke to sweat-soaked pajamas and a bad headache. At eight fifteen I called Melanie. "I feel awful."

"Covid?" she asked.

"Yeah, I think."

"Oh, Stan."

"Afraid I'm going down."

"You have medicines?"

"Thanks, Mel. I don't need anything. Oh crap, I may have infected you."

"Yeah." She took in a long breath. "I'll have to quarantine."

"Sorry, Mel. I've tried to be careful."

"Chicken soup," she said. I could tell she was doing her best to be cheery.

"No need, thanks."

"I'll pick some up at the deli on the way to my afternoon job. —Oh yeah, I won't be able to go to that job. Anyway, I'm bringing you the soup."

"With any luck, I'll be asleep." She wanted to help. I knew I should let her. "All right, Florence Nightingale. I'll put a key under the mat."

I put the key out and called Hannah. "I'll be off the case for a couple of days."

There was a short silence, then, "You said you were making progress."

"We are."

"Are you coming by tonight? I'd really like that."

"No, I can't."

"I thought you and I were having fun, Stan. Then you got weird on me the other night."

"I'm sick, Hannah. I'm coming down with it."

"Oh, sorry. Bud's still working the case, right?"

"Sure." At least I thought he might be.

"Too bad, you're going to miss my new swimsuit."

"Yeah, too bad."

"Get better," she said, sounding bored. I wondered if she worried about me—but only for a few moments as I fell asleep.

I woke when the lock clacked on the front door. Melanie appeared in the bedroom doorway, wearing a khaki shirt, gray surgical gloves and a pale orange mask.

She held a take-out bag. "You awake?"

I rolled onto my side to get a better look at her.

"Yeah."

"Want some soup?"

"No thanks."

"It's still warm."

"I am too," I said.

She set the soup on the floor and headed toward me.

I held up a hand to warn her off. "I don't want you catching it."

"Do you have a thermometer?"

"No. Please don't come so close. Please."

She stopped short, reached into her handbag and brought out a paper. "Bud left this at the office, along with a flash drive."

"It can wait."

"I think Bud's gone looking for Jacob Christian."

"What?"

"The note says he's off to follow a lead. He left me a note too, asking me to research cases of preachers murdered by their mothers." She chuckled. "You know Bud."

Nutty Bud, like Don Quixote following some conspiracy dream. I took a deep breath, and it felt all right. If my lungs stayed in shape, I'd be okay. "Good. He won't come bother me."

Mel stood there watching. "Since I can't go to my afternoon job, can I use the office?"

"Sure, Mel."

"Call me if you need anything. Anytime. Okay?"

"Yeah, Mel. All I need is sleep."

IT WAS DARK OUTSIDE. My clock said, 8:18. My head beat a lumberjack chop. I drifted in and out of merciful sleep, thinking of Bud, thinking of Covid. Maybe Bud would find Jake Christian and get Hannah out of my life. That would be for the best, wouldn't it?

Dreaming of trying to find a toilet, desperate. Waking, *really* not wanting to get up. I slid to the side of the bed, dull pain in all my joints. I forced myself to sit upright. Definitely Covid-19.

"Hold on, Stan." It was Mel's voice. She wore her mask and gloves and popped one of those clear plastic shields over her face. Where had she found that?

"I'll help."

"You can't do this, Mel. You'll get sick."

"I want to—"

"Back away." Loud, I spoke too loud. "I *will* make it to the bathroom on my own." She gave me space.

I got back from the bathroom and gingerly climbed into bed. Mel brought me some of the soup. I frowned at her. "You kept my key."

She looked pleased with herself. "You going to call the cops?"

Mel set me up with the soup and then lingered by the bedroom door. "I'm staying tonight."

I felt a bit shocked and more than a little touched, reassured … and worried.

"Not in here," she said. "In your guest room, if that's okay. I opened the window and turned on a fan." I didn't answer and she said, "People die of this disease. We aren't letting that happen to you."

"I'm not dying, Mel. I'm only thirty-nine. I've barely even coughed." But I was breathing hard after a twenty-foot walk to the bathroom and a climb into bed.

"I'm not just helping you. I can't go home and endanger my mom. Can't stay with my sister. Shouldn't go to a hotel either." She shook her head. "Honestly, Stan, I have nowhere else."

"Oh, yeah, Mel. Some date I was." I tried to think what a healthy guy might say. "You stole my key and now you invite yourself for a slumber party." I paused for a few seconds, hoping she might laugh and said, "Mi casa es su casa." I set the soup bowl on the night table and curled into a fetal cocoon.

In my half-sleep I pictured Hannah in a white gown at the senior prom, and then naked, splashing water at me in Harry's Pond that night. She surfaced at the side of her swimming pool and gave me the finger. I heard her apathetic, "Get better," when I told her I had Covid.

Then, Mel drifted in with gentle kindness, serving chicken soup.

CHAPTER 35

JEFF

Late September 2020, Redondo Beach CA and New Mexico

Things were really fucked up. Hannah had kicked him out last month. —Not all his fault; he'd betrayed her, but only after she'd treated him like a fool. He'd rented this lousy apartment with views of a parking lot and urban sprawl. His business partner disdained him. The pandemic was killing people left and right. The President mocked basic health precautions and threatened to ignore the election results.

His past taunted him night and day.

It wasn't about Suzi. Jeff barely remembered her. It wasn't about mutilating his hands or about deceiving all those clueless people. It wasn't about Ruby, not directly.

It was about his deteriorating mental state and the fact that he didn't know if half of his visions were dreams or wakeful hallucinations. The last time he'd visited Hannah, they'd tried for make-up sex. Opening his eyes in the height of ecstasy, he found his mother, writhing like a serpent, beneath him. She reached up to stroke his temple. "You don't need that whore, Jeff. You have me." He'd recoiled in horror, thrown on his pants, and fled.

It was about Luke, too, his son who deserved a better father. And Ellen, the newswoman he'd met, who'd thrilled Jeff in bed, until Luke walked in and caught them. How could Jeff, kept so innocent by his mother, have known better than any of this? Didn't that innocence and natural born lust exculpate his guilt? —God Damn it, no. His mother had taught the catechism of deceit, forbidden his physical needs and almost convinced him he was Jesus incarnate. But he couldn't blame her anymore.

He drank a straight shot of cheap gin and two beers, sat in his armchair and watched the news on TV. They showed a clip from a Trump rally. Infuriating! Leaning back, breathing deep, he tried to let it go. Then *he* was on stage, not this president. Not ranting about imagined conspiracies, but about his mother piercing the palms of his hands with that sharp, little knife. Holding up his hands, he shouted to the crowd, "She stole these from me. My youth, my sexual adventures … even my precious skin."

Crazy irony: the president of the United States employed the same tactics to excite the crowd, as Jeff and his mother had before, as Jeff used to sell fake artifacts from India to unwary customers. Tell them anything—*We will heal you.* Tell them again. Elaborate—*My son has divine power.* Repeat, until they think it might be true. Bring in people to lie for you. *Watch Jeff cure these people in wheelchairs.* Say it louder. Those who contradict are the spawn of Satan. *Charlatans;* call them out before they're able to hang that tag on you. A time-honored strategy that worked on a certain type of person.

Jeff felt a presence beside him and turned to see Ruby, alive and well, still his faithful companion, watching TV with him.

Your president is quite a funny guy, she said. This time Ruby had a male voice, sounded like Joe Biden.

He blew out a loud breath. He needed to calm down, distract his mind, focus on anything that might be real. On an impulse, he went on the internet and typed his mother's name. The results stole his breath: "Faith healer, Sarah Lamb, returns." He read the piece over twice. The Lord's Chapel near Miami; Jeff remembered the place from their ministry. His mother had made friends with some of the church elders, especially that scam artist, Bob Smithfield. Smithfield had gone on the road with them back then. He'd arranged their phony healing routine. Now returned from Indonesia, according to the article, Sarah Lamb had somehow become pastor of that church. Two months ago! She'd been back in the US for six months! How had he missed this?

Holy God. Holy God. Holy God. Jeff's ears were ringing. He felt his brain expanding, pressing against his skull. He heard Dr. Newhart, say, "Now it's time to return to your peaceful place."

JEFF JUMPED INTO HIS BRONCO and drove east, fast as he dared. Passing red rock cliffs west of Gallup, NM, Ruby insinuated herself into his day, with that beautiful collie snout of hers. She sat upright on the passenger seat, brown and white, sleek fur, her mouth open, tongue lapping the air, tail wagging. *Pretty here, isn't it?* she said. *You're coming to see me at the cabin, right? Please, please, PLEASE.*

Goddamn, Ruby had Hannah's voice this time.

Eyes on the road, the dog said.

Jeff was doing 75, headed for a ditch. He jacked the wheel and swerved back onto pavement.

JEFF WOKE IN THE NIGHT, startled. *Breathe. Breathe. If you can breathe, you don't have Covid.* That was new. When had Covid begun permeating every conscious moment? Moonlight shone in through the window, and he realized where he was; in his mother's old bed at the cabin. Jesus! The picture of the Lord stared at him from the bookshelf. The healthy Ruby filled his dreams that night. *Thanks for coming back to see me,* she said. *I don't want to trouble you, but I do get lonely.*

The next morning, with clearer thoughts and a cup of coffee, Jeff stood beside Ruby's grave, gazing over the rolling terrain toward Colorado. He loved this lonely mesa, as much as he feared its mystic power. He craved and loathed the memories. No need to rush back to California. He drove to Gallup and kept his distance from people in the stores, as he stocked up. Using the Wi-Fi at McDonalds on old US Highway 66 and the disguised internet portal he'd created, he sent emails to Hannah, Malik and Luke:

Off to India and Indonesia. Buying for the business. Sorry I didn't say goodbye before I left.

He gathered firewood and cooked a steak on the grill. After eating, he poked his left hand with the greasy steak knife until it yielded a drop. Ruby gave him a disapproving doggy glower.

A WEEK ON THE MESA. Still no closer to self-knowledge, if that was what he wanted. He went online in Gallup and ordered new Hindi statues and elephant carvings from a merchant in India. He sent an email to Malik bragging about his *finds*. Still on the computer, he checked the latest Covid news. Nine hundred deaths just yesterday in the US, disease rampant in the Navajo Nation. Insidious germs permeating the air, microbes closing in. Jeff scrutinized the people leaving McDonalds, all of them inhaling and exhaling. He felt a little better, when he couldn't spot any germs billowing out of them.

CHAPTER 36

OCTOBER 10-20, 2020, NEW MEXICO

Another week went by. Ruby slept with him at night, curled by his feet. He invented a story to explain a longer absence—a passionate love affair with an Indian beauty—fun to imagine. He slipped that fiction into an email to his partner, Sirjay. *I'll be sailing slowly toward Indonesia with my lover.*

Every day, despite Covid—he couldn't help himself—Jeff left the safety of the cabin and drove to Gallup or Grants. He double masked his face, donned gloves and bought coffee at McDonalds. He could see the germs now, minuscule as they were, spewing from the cashiers' mouth when she said, "Should I leave space for cream?"

He took the coffee outside, where he could breathe, and checked the news online. Every night in bed, he revisited his sins as he drifted toward sleep. Malik confronted him; "Why are there no elephants in this shipment?" Hannah derided his "used car salesman mindset." What about Hannah's deceiving soul? What about her manipulating Luke to take her side? What about the way she used to lick inside his ear to tickle him? He missed that playful intimacy.

ONLINE AT MCDONALDS Jeff ordered Indonesian *artifacts* for the store and sent an update to Malik. Fascinating the way a guy could set up internet service to mimic email arriving from far off places. Life was an illusion, after all. All except Ruby. She seldom spoke these days, but she was more real to him than anything on the internet.

Checking *Sarah Lamb* on Google, the results set his gut crawling: *Florida Preacher to Congregation, "Embrace Covid-19 as a Friend."* It wasn't the first article about a minister defying good sense. It was the article's next line: *Sarah Lamb, famed evangelist from the nineties, reappeared in Miami's suburbs earlier this year, preaching the gospel of defiance.* The story went on with quotes like, *The blood of God, it heals us. … Those who are innocent, God will protect. … For those who trust not, for those who cower in their homes and shun His holy churches, refuge shall be denied.*

Goddamn it. Does she want to kill them all? Jeff dumped his coffee in the trash, strode to Discount Liquors, and purchased a pint of gin and cans of tonic water. With gin in one cup-holder of his Bronco and tonic in the other, he drove Interstate 40, alternating swigs. He turned north, headed for the cabin. The red rocks on either side began to blur as he drove. Ruby's face, the face of a mummified doggy corpse, loomed in his windshield. His body jerked, and he nearly ran the Bronco off the road.

Take it easy, Master. Slow down.

Shit, he hated that version of Ruby.

Stop the car, she barked.

Jeff pulled onto a dirt patch and drank the last of the gin. He leaned back and pondered. A few of the Navajo's sheep strolled near and gave him a once-over.

Ruby's carcass floated in his vision—grotesque. *Your mom will make all those Jesus-lovers sick. She's yours, Jeff, your momma. You got to control her. You can't ask a dog to handle your business.*

"You mean kill her?" he asked.

No way! Collies detest capital punishment. Tie her down someplace, till the Virus turns to plain old snot.

When he was halfway sober, Jeff drove on. At the cabin, he lay in his mother's bed.

Control her. Tie her down.

Falling in and out of sleep. In his dream his mother shouted, "Spread the disease and die." The people in the pews chanted, "Die. Die. Die."

My responsibility to stop her … Responsibility is such bull shit.

It was dark and cold. Stars shone outside the window.

Go to Florida and confront her.

Ruby chimed in. *Make the bitch come to you.*

The next day, back on the internet, he looked up Sarah Lamb's latest sermon, titled, "Our Savior Can Not Sin." It was about Donald Trump and his mission to save America. Spreading disease, spreading lies. That old buzzing filled Jeff's ears, but he had to focus. Inspired by his favorite dream and by Ruby's instructions, he ordered what he needed on the internet, sent to *Jeff Lamb, General Delivery, Crownpoint NM.*

With his dog at his side, he explored the old uranium mine borings he'd seen in the area as a teenager and chose the best one. On the Florida Lord's Chapel website, beneath his mother's smiling picture, he clicked the little box, *Contact Reverend Lamb.* The email he sent read, "It's Jeff, Mom. Come see me. You know where."

Chapter 37

October 24, 2020

A few days later, his mother arrived.

Jeff double masked and opened the door.

She wore a gold-color blouse and black tights, blond still, but her skin was deeply tanned and wrinkled.

He folded his arms to conceal his shaky hands. "Step back, Mother, twelve feet."

She snorted a laugh and stood her ground.

"You have the Virus. I know you do."

She pushed past him into the cabin. "Don't be ridiculous, son. The Lord protects me."

Let her infect me, he thought. *It's the end I deserve. As long as I take her down too.*

She gave him a so-what shrug and a condescending smirk, as she handed him a small white bag. "Here, I brought pastries."

The bitch can still make me tremble. He took the bag and set it on the desk.

They stood, facing each other.

"I'm not going to wear one of those either." She gestured at the masks on his face.

Smiling now, like the picture on the church's website, like his old *momma*—adoring and holy—she spread her arms. She looked up to the heavens. "Thank you, Lord. You've brought my son home."

She does want me. She's thanking God.

She beckoned, and he couldn't help himself. Without conscious effort, his arms enfolded her. Holding her, looking over her shoulder, he was shocked to see the dead, grotesque Ruby, her empty eye sockets glaring. *I'm a dog, and I wouldn't hug HER.* Ruby turned her back on him and hunkered in the corner.

That afternoon Jeff and his mother opened a three-day dialogue. He sat at the desk and she in the armchair.

"Where have you been, Mother? I searched in Indonesia."

She laughed. "Foolish boy. I was far from there with some fine people. I found new love with Jesus and my man, Cedric. I even smoked."

Fine people? Cedric? Smoking?

"I waited here for three months, Jeff, but you didn't return. Without our ministry, I felt lost. Then God told me, 'Get out of the dark tunnel of your sorrow and act.'"

Her eyes looked past Jeff. She smiled a wistful smile. "I began to dream, thank God. My dreams filled up with islands, beautiful native people sipping drinks from coconut shells under palm trees. I thought they were in Indonesia, but they weren't.

"I was on a train to Florida to tell Bob Smithfield my plans for Indonesia. In the lounge car, the most beautiful man caught my eye. He wore a saffron yellow robe with brown swirls on it. His skin was a lovely cafe-au-lait. His golden-brown eyes seduced me. His hair was a brown tangle. There was something holy about him. I knew right then; God had sent him to me."

She was my inspiration and my guide, Jeff thought.

Ruby finished the thought: *No wonder you're fucked up.*

"'I'm Cedric,' he said. 'Sit here, beautiful womon.' I liked the way he said, 'womon' instead of woman. I sat in the train seat facing him, and I told him about our ministry, the revival meetings you and I held … the way you'd deserted me. I didn't think I would, but I cried. Cedric reached across and dried my cheeks with his handkerchief."

His mother stood and gave Jeff a guilt-provoking pout.

Phooey.

She came close, and Jeff flinched. She pulled a muffin from the bag on the desk, took a bite and offered him the rest.

Germs! He pushed her hand aside and backed away.

"*Chicken.*" She went outside and tossed the muffin toward one of the pinion pines. "You may not appreciate it, but the birds will."

Jeff followed, as she strolled toward the edge of the mesa, her blond hair and her golden blouse sparkling in the sunshine.

He could push her off the cliff, but that would offend Ruby.

"I told Cedric I was looking for a place where people worship simply and sincerely. I mentioned Indonesia. 'Womon, you be abandoned by your son, I t'ink, but not by God.' Cedric said that to me. 'Come to Jamaica wit' me. The best revival meetin's we have there; not those dump-dog, tight-ass America kind. We drum all night. We dance. We sing. We smoke ganja till the air is all smog up. We praise God with our passion-ate voices.'

"Cedric had a beautiful aura. Lovely creases fanned by his eyes. Dark freckles flecked his cheeks. —Older than I'd thought, but still the most handsome man. When he called American revivals, 'dump-dog,' I thought, *Yes, perhaps they are.* I agreed to go with him, and a month later we married."

Jeff was dumbstruck. He had a stepfather! Finally, he said, "You've been preaching with him?"

"No. Cedric was very clear that a woman could not lead."

"And smoking marijuana?"

"Ganja. Cedric wanted me to."

Jeff snorted.

"You may not remember, son; I was very obedient to your father when he was alive, just as the bible instructs. Cedric taught me; ganja is a holy herb. We were very happy."

"Why come back to Florida?"

"God sent me messages, son. My country needed me. Now that I'm back, you and I can preach again. We'll go beyond, to heal people all over the world."

They stood near Ruby's grave now. The dog sat atop it, shaking her desiccated head in disbelief.

"You weren't as good at preaching as I'd hoped," his mother said. "We'll work on your technique. Maybe you'll change your mind and show them a little blood."

"We aren't going to do that, Mother." Jeff showed her his almost scar-free palms.

"Oh Jeff! You've disfigured yourself."

They strolled back and entered the cabin, and never discussed their mission again. But their talks went on and on, becoming repetitious, especially when they discussed Covid-19:

"You're killing people, Mother. They need to shelter at home and protect themselves, not sing together in a church full of germs."

"So melodramatic, son. Our Lord and I are saving people."

He tried again and again to convince her, until he ground his teeth and changed the subject.

Questions popped up:

"How did you take over that church in Florida, mother?"

"Just like back in Oklahoma, Jeff. The pastor was a weakling. I was strong. I had help, too, Bob Smithfield. He's president of that church board."

"Smithfield," Jeff said. "Yeah, he's a real son of a bitch."

"*Swearing*, son. You know I don't like that."

"I'm not your puppet anymore."

"Oh, yes you are."

Maybe she was right. Jeff couldn't tell what he was anymore.

Trump is a damned phony, Mother. How can you support his bull shit?"

"If it's BS, Jeff, it's *holy* excrement. Donald is making America safe for Christianity."

His mother made a face every time he swore, and Jeff did it often those three days.

During each of their discussions, he contemplated poisoning her or slitting her throat, starving her, as she had done to Ruby. When she went to the bathroom, he removed the butcher knife from its drawer and ran his finger along the sharp edge. He heard a soft whine, spotted Ruby watching from the corner, and put the knife away.

CHAPTER 38

Disgusting. Infuriating, useless. There was no reasoning with her.

That third night, in his room, Jeff brought out the bottle of liquor he'd stashed under the bed, Southern Comfort. He drank straight from the bottle, just feet from the bathroom where Ruby had died. He kept his eyes closed, so he wouldn't see the collie, but he felt her scrutinizing him. The syrupy booze made him queasy, but he finished the half-pint. Jeff's old shrink stopped by in a vision and asked him, *How do you feel about this interaction with your Mother Wound.*

"Shitty, Doc; I want to kill her." He pictured her body at the bottom of one of those old pits he'd seen in the desert.

You're getting crazier, the shrink said. *That's quite helpful.* Dr. Newhart pursed his lips, the way he did when he was thinking, and asked, *Did you notice that your mother never asked about your life?*

Life was about dying and moving on. Even Covid was about that, so if his mother died …

Ruby growled softly, and he opened his eyes. She sat by the door to the bathroom, looking much the worse for her morbid state. *If you murder her, she'll haunt you.*

The dog's right, Jeff thought. *I picture her body in the mine shaft, but it doesn't have to be dead.*

The next morning, he opened the box that he'd received from Amazon the previous week. The Elvis jacket—white with silver sequins, like in his dreams—sparkled. He put on a pair of jeans, the jacket, and white gloves. He slipped a vial of date-rape drug that he'd ordered elsewhere online inside one glove.

He smiled like her adoring son, as he came out, singing, *"Are you lonesome tonight?"* She wore a pale blue jogging suit this morning, her blond hair neatly combed. She rose from the armchair, delighted. "Jeff, you finally look happy. And that outfit. You're going to do it! You're going to preach with me, aren't you?" She hugged him tight for a long half minute. "Thank you, Jeff. We'll be so happy."

Inside his head different music—*Please release me. Let me go.* He walked to the kitchen counter and pulled out two glasses.

"I'll pour some wine to celebrate. Or orange juice; would you rather?"

"This is special. I could have a little wine."

He brought it to her, and she sipped, smiling over the rim of the glass at him, sipped again.

USING BENNY BEGAY'S TRUCK with the winch, the tarps and ropes he'd bought, Jeff deposited her where she couldn't harm anyone. He could keep her alive down there for months, until the pandemic subsided … feeding her canned food, like a dog.

That should have made him laugh, but levity eluded him.

Jeff parked his mother's rental car at the Gallup train station and hitch-hiked home.

Now that his mother was safely stowed, Jeff's dreams grew tranquil. Ruby offered no comments. She appeared only in her downy, brown-and-white coat and slept peacefully on his bed each night.

CHAPTER 39

BUD

November 3, Election Day

I checked in to a Comfort Inn in Gallup NM. That Tuesday afternoon, I found the McKinley County Assessor's Office. A plain paper sign on one of the double glass doors said, *All Persons Entering MUST Wear a Mask.*

"Sure, you pricks." I strapped it on and went in. On a computer there, I located a parcel outside a town called Crownpoint, still owned by Sarah Lamb. Bud Randolph, crack detective!

November 4

THE NEXT MORNING, I watched the news. Fake! No way Biden won Arizona. No way the SOB was gaining like that in those other states. Trump said he'd won, and he had. The steal was on, and I was pissed!

I threw the plat maps from the land office onto the passenger seat and headed out. An hour later, I was hunting for the right crappy dirt road to follow. I drove past some of those unusual Indian—excuse me, *Native American*—round dwellings and a few plain houses. People stared. A guy in a dirty blue pickup truck followed for a ways and then dropped back. Gravel banged against the bottom of my Mustang, wounding my sweet car. Stan would pay for that, goddamn it.

Finally, at one fork, near the top of the mesa, I veered right, drove a few dozen feet and halted. The so-called road was eating the Mustang's lunch, and I was close now. I trekked the last five minutes and came to a green Ford Bronco at the end of the road with a red gas can clamped to the back tailgate, California license plates. Jake's.

I walked between some of those scrubby, little pine trees and spotted the cabin. Its porch all crooked; it needed a coat of paint and some repairs.

There was a window beside the front door, dirty glass. Inside, I saw a grungy room with a bed, a kitchen area in back, a closed door leading to a bathroom maybe. No one in sight. I walked back along the side of the cabin and heard the front door creak open. A man with a shaggy, brown beard came around the corner and gawked at me. "What are you doing here?"

"Jake Christian?" I studied the guy for a second. The beard wasn't much of a disguise. "I'm Bud Randolph. Your wife, Hannah, is looking for you."

The fellow gave a phony smile, but didn't reach to shake my hand. "Not Jake. My name's Jeff."

"Jeff Lamb, then. Is Sarah here too?"

The guy's eyes went all wide. *Surprise!*

"Your mother, Sarah," I said. "I know your secrets."

Jake/Jeff shot me an *oh-shit,* grimace. "Yeah, well … give me a minute to mask up and then come in. I bet you're thirsty."

CHAPTER 40

STAN

November 3- 5, Manhattan Beach CA

Melanie brought me tea in the morning. She wore her full pandemic face gear, plus that ruby stud earring in her left ear, and a pale pink tee shirt.

I straightened, planning to sit up in bed. My back and shoulders ached. I pushed through it, thinking that moving might help. It didn't. The tea felt good going down.

Mel retreated to the doorway again. "I was pushy yesterday when I took over your guest room."

I tried to think through the brain fog the disease was creating. "That's okay, Mel. I owe you."

"My sister's taking care of Mom, but I worry. Mom's in her seventies and vulnerable."

"You can tell me about it if you like."

She looked away. "You may have noticed; I don't do much *personal*."

"For the same reason you wear those glasses?"

"I'm not wearing them with you."

"And now that tee shirt."

"I should cover up?"

"No. Please. It's the only good thing ..." *The one thing that makes me want to keep my eyes open.*

She crossed her arms over her chest. "I thought about this for a while. Like the glasses. I gave myself permission with you."

"I'm glad, Mel. You should always ... You could have lots of guys interested, if you let them see you."

"I told you; jerks swarm like ants all over this city."

After I finished, she took the tea cup back to the kitchen and then headed for the office.

As I drifted off to sleep, my mind took in the truth: *Mel lets me see her because I'm harmless.*

I thought of Hannah too. I could have been with her tonight in the pool, ignoring the fact that she had a husband who might be dead. Maybe it was fantasy, but when Hannah locked eyes with me, I felt anything but *harmless.* I felt daring.

Covid was screwing everything up.

MEL WAS BACK wearing her PPE gear that evening, armed with a thermometer. I protested, but she came close. She helped me prop up with pillows and stuck the thermometer under my tongue. She went out and returned with a bowl of water and a washcloth.

She read my temperature. "Not bad."

"How not bad?"

"One-oh-two point three." She dabbed my face with the cool, damp washcloth. "How does this feel?"

"Really good, Mel." She laid the cloth back in the basin and began unbuttoning my pajama top, watching my reaction with those deep brown eyes.

"*Mel,* you're getting pretty forward."

She laughed, which made me feel a little better. She wrung out the washcloth and wiped down my chest. "When my papa was ill, my sister and I took turns bathing him." There was a little catch in her voice, which told me that her dad had died afterwards. She left the room and returned with a metal tank.

"What, now, Mel?"

"Oxygen. I raided my mom's medical supplies." She set the tank down near the bed and began fastening a tube to the regulator.

"I thought you weren't going to your mom's place."

"I didn't, actually. My sister picked it up and brought it to the office. And don't worry; Mom has plenty. She hoards oxygen like Bud does T. P."

"I don't need it."

She gave me a look like Nurse Ratched. "Actually, you do. Clip this under your nose." She turned on the oxygen. My breaths came easier, and I realized she was right.

NOVEMBER 4

EARLY IN THE EVENING I asked Mel about the election. Her smiling eyes were great medicine. "They're still counting votes, but Biden's gaining ground. He won Arizona, which is big."

Wonderful.

"Trump demanded they stop counting while he was ahead."

"Of course he did." No surprise; Trump had telegraphed that move before the election.

"Get better, and we'll celebrate together."

"Super idea, Mel." I dropped back to sleep.

Hannah appeared in my dreams, lying next to me in bed, stroking my chest, stealthily lifting the covers. I thought she had intimate intentions, but a barber's razor appeared in her hand, open and ready to slice. That sure woke me up.

NOVEMBER 5

MEL CAME IN MASK-LESS and sat on the side of my bed.

"No, Mel."

"It's all right, Stan. I got my test back." So, she had Covid too.

"I'm so sorry."

"It's not from you, Stan. I had the test three days ago, and it takes time for the virus to develop. I get tested every week for my mom's sake."

"Could be from Bud." We both said that at the same time and smiled at each other.

"Have you heard from him, Mel?"

"He sent a vague text on Tuesday, which mentioned Gallup NM. Nothing the last two days. At least we know where he went."

"He's probably sulking about the election." *She has Covid, so I can touch her,* I thought. I reached out and held her hand. "You look good, Mel. Are you okay?"

"Yeah. I had a little headache last two days, nothing too bad. Think I'm going to be one of the lucky ones."

I raised her hand and kissed it. "You're very kind to me."

She gave me a terrific smile and touched my arm. "You smell like a grizzly bear. You able to take a shower?"

I didn't want to stink around her so I managed it. Mel made my bed and laid out my PJs. After a few minutes, she came back in and sat on the side of the bed.

"Mel, have you been flirting with me?"

"Is that okay?"

"Absolutely. I like this side of you."

Flirting was only a game for women; I knew that. A gorgeous woman like Mel, even one who barricaded herself behind heavy glasses, would never want more than that with ordinary me. (Wasn't that true for Hannah too?)

"You're not my boss here. We're just friends taking care of each other." She watched me for a minute. "I used to flirt, but I mostly gave it up."

CHAPTER 41

November 6

Sometimes I lay awake, between long spells of sleep, thinking idle thoughts, like, *What was it that made me fall for Hannah back in high school?* Memories came then—Hannah the cheerleader, short skirt, great legs that launched her acrobatic leaps; Hannah dancing with abandon at parties, giggling between swigs of tequila and wet kisses. None of the memories had anything to do with generosity or caring. Loyalty had gone out the window that next year when she'd left for college.

It was dark outside. I sat up in bed and checked my cell phone. No messages from Hannah or Bud. Mel entered my room wearing yellow pajamas.

"You were asleep when I got here, so I made myself comfortable. Joe Biden's ahead in Georgia and Pennsylvania."

"Fantastic."

She came over and laid a palm on my forehead. "Not too hot today."

"Hear anything from Bud?"

She shook her head. "I stopped by his apartment and spoke with the landlady through the security screen door. She said that Bud's been gone for days. ... Then she gave me one of those *looks*."

I waited.

"You know, the *You got no business around here,* stare-down." Mel looked indignant.

"Sorry," I said. "By the way, has Hannah Christian called the office to ask about me?"

"Not a peep." She headed for the door but turned back. "Before you ask, I checked Bud's credit accounts again. The most recent were for meals on Tuesday in Gallup. No charges for gas, so he's not headed home."

When Mel returned with some leftover Chinese food for me, I asked, "You ever drive a motorhome?"

"Where's this going, Stan?"

"I have to look for Bud. I can't take a plane, and I don't think I can drive that far."

"You need more time to recover."

"He's my Army pal. I promised Cheryl I'd take care of him."

She shook her head. "You can't even care for yourself."

"That's why I'm asking you. You're the only one I know with Covid-19 *and* a driver's license."

"Thanks a lot." She touched my hand for a second. "It is kind of nice to be co-contagious, but a motorhome?"

"We can't eat at restaurants or stay in motels. We *can* go on the road."

"My sister could pick up the motorhome for me. *Instacart* can bring us food for the trip. Cold cuts, hummus, bread, veggies …"

The idea of hummus didn't excite me, but I said, "You're a resourceful woman, Mel. I like that."

"Thanks. That's all you like?" She gave me a bright smile. I grazed my hand down her arm. Her sense of humor, her brown eyes and that body I was just discovering, were also on the list of likes.

"We'd better wait a couple of days," she said.

"I'm doing better, and I can't put this off. If you won't take me—"

She felt my forehead again and nodded. "Bud's a jerk, but he's our jerk. ... Okay. If your temperature isn't too high, we'll leave tomorrow."

CHAPTER 42

JEFF

November 4

Jeff had lowered supplies down to his mom three times in the week since he'd stowed her in the pit.

One morning, while brushing his teeth, he heard a sound outside. A deer rambling past? He walked out, looked around the corner of the cabin and saw a not-so-tall, red-faced guy, snooping.

What the hell?

The fellow wore one of those khaki shirts with two button-down pockets. Jeff looked for Ruby, but she was nowhere in sight. Some watch dog! He took a breath and faced the man. "What are you doing here?"

"Jake Christian?" the guy asked. He gave Jeff a good once-over and nodded. "I'm Bud Randolph. Your wife, Hannah, is looking for you."

Jeff swallowed hard and tried to look sincere. "Not Jake. My name's Jeff."

"Jeff Lamb, then. Is Sarah here too?"

Holy Shit!

The guy grinned at him. "Your mother, Sarah. I know your secrets."

Shit, Shit, Triple Shit! "Yeah, well … Give me a minute to put on a mask and then come in. I bet you're thirsty."

In his bedroom, he grabbed not only a mask, but also the little vial of sleepy-time drug. What other choice did he have?

CHAPTER 43

BUD

November 4, 2020

I opened my eyes, blinked a few times, and saw dirt walls closing in. At the top, maybe 30 feet up, was a metal frame with a pulley. Some sort of damned well? A woman's voice from close by— "I bet you have a headache."

What the hell? I felt a tarp under me, covering something lumpy; gravel? Sore. My shoulders and my back felt like crap. My head throbbed.

"Want some water?" the woman asked. "Sit up, and I'll get you some."

I crawled to the gritty wall and leaned against it. The woman came over and handed me a plastic bottle. She settled her butt on the tarp where I'd been lying.

My vision was blurry. "Who are you?"

"I'm Sarah. Sip slowly."

I closed my eyes and must have blacked out. It was darker when I came to. I managed to stand, a little shaky, leaning against the wall, which was sand and gravel, like the floor. I looked up. It was a long way to the top. *This is some fucking development.* I dug my knuckles into the wall and a handful of gravelly crud crumbled down. Could a guy get a foothold in that?

The woman, *Sarah*, stood a few feet away. I squinted at her. Jake Christian's mother's name was … I'd seen pictures of Sarah Lamb, but this Sarah was older, time-worn, still blond, a little taller than me, I guessed. Hard to tell with her standing over me.

"You're that preacher woman, Jake's mother, right?"

"I'm *Jeff's* mother. My son has insulted your dignity by dumping you here. I apologize."

What a crazy pickle, down a well with a famous evangelist. "You went off to Indonesia and then came back to Florida, right?"

"You've been deceived." She smirked. "I don't know what to call you."

"Call me Bud. Not Indonesia?"

"No."

"Then where?"

"None of your business, is it?"

Feisty bitch. "Your Jeff was calling himself Jacob. I caught up to him in a cabin on the mesa." Shit. I'd been drugged. But how? Jake/Jeff had popped the can of iced tea open and handed it over. No glass to drink from, no chance to add anything. –But the bastard had.

She chuckled, "Jacob? How biblical. That's my old cabin, where you found him. We used it as a refuge in those days. Jeff ran away from me." She murmured the last few words, barely audible. "Now he's confined me … us.

"Drink slowly," she said. "Don't be scared. Jeff's a good boy. He provides water and food. If you call Spam and canned pinto beans food."

I noticed a stench and wondered if the pinto beans had caused Sarah Lamb to pollute that fucking hole.

"If you're wondering how he got you down here," Sarah said. "He bundled you in that tarp and lowered you on a rope." Still watching me, she said, "The smell is from damp earth and my latrine over there." I looked where she was pointing and saw only more sand.

"We're living in natural kitty litter. Good for covering human waste." She used an empty tin can to scoop up some gravel and dump it. She smiled as if it was okay to be stuck in that shithole.

God damn it. I looked up again. It was tight in there, the walls ready to collapse. If a monster rain came, what then? I reached for my cellphone in my back pocket—gone.

"Jeff provides all the necessities, even this little propane heater. I raised him civilized." Sarah's chuckle might have been a cackle or even a sob.

"How'd you end up here?" I asked.

"He sent me a message in Florida, and I rushed to him. I thought he wanted to preach with me again. Instead, he screamed at me that I was killing people by telling them to come to church and sing the Lord's praise. *How could he?* We argued. Then he medicated me and dropped me here."

She looked so pitiful, I thought of comforting her, touching her arm maybe, but what comfort could there be? "Do people in Florida know where you went?"

"I'd never divulge my cabin." She stared straight at me, her shoulders shaking with her sobs. "Jeff would know that. ... Before you ask anything else, please tell me. The election must be over. Donald won, didn't he? God would have it no other way."

She was right of course, even though the pricks on CNN, and even Fox News said it was too close to call. "He won, but the bastards want to steal the election."

"The forces of evil try to beguile us, but we don't have to join them." Mostly, her voice oozed sweetness, but it turned insistent just then. "Please do not swear in my presence."

"Yeah. I guess they're evil. Trump won't let them get away with it. You have another bottle of water?" She handed it over, and I guzzled.

"They've already stolen God from the schools," she said. "They invented a fake virus to keep us from our worship."

Yeah, yeah, yeah. "There's food here somewhere?"

"I'll open a can of corn for you." She picked it up and showed me. "Whatever drug Jeff gave us, your stomach's not ready for meat." She used a can opener on the corn and handed it over along with a fork. "We have canned chicken for later."

That actually didn't sound bad. I took a forkful of corn. "Your son really provided for us." Another bite. "A real prince." A mouthful, trying not to cram it down too fast. "My favorite Spam flavor is Jalapeño. How about you?"

I saw her nose wrinkle in the dimming light. "My favorite Spam is porterhouse steak."

So Sarah Lamb had a sense of humor. Good, since I was stuck with her. I gulped down the last of the corn, thinking that maybe I could jam empty cans into the wall to make steps.

Sarah said, "We were talking about evil-doers and Donald's mission. Perhaps you'll let me elaborate."

At least I'd landed in a pit with someone who appreciated the president. "Go for it."

"God sent Donald to save our sinful land. You understand?"

"That's your theory. It's not why I support him."

"With a man like Donald, you must not only support, but idolize him."

"I like Trump a lot, but really? He came from God?"

"Then what do you think?"

I asked myself a funny question: *If you're stuck in a place with only a religious nut job for company, do you play along?* "Maybe I'll tell you later. Do we have a lot of these empty cans?"

Sarah pointed to a pile I hadn't noticed.

I looked over the walls trying to find a place that sloped outward. Using a full can of beans as a hammer, I drove the empty corn container into the dirt wall. Sara brought a few empties over, and I jammed another one in to the left of the first, and then two more a foot higher.

Sarah stood back watching me, and I said, "Wish me luck."

Leaning close to the wall, I set my right foot on the first can, stepped my left onto the can beside it, eased myself up.

They held my weight!

I edged my foot to one of the higher cans and shifted slowly. The can gave and dumped me on my ass. Lying there, breathing, thinking that maybe I just had to be more careful, maybe when I wasn't still woozy from the drugs … I tried really hard to believe this could work.

"When it's light tomorrow and I'm feeling better, I'll get us out of here."

Sarah moved back to her tarp, and I lay on mine, pulling a blanket over me. It grew dark. Sarah fired up the propane heater. Its glow allowed me a little vision. Did I want to tell her? Why not?

"I had a job at a GM plant in Doraville, Georgia till it closed in oh-eight. Best job, a guy could want. Good wages. Honest work. Great friends. We played softball after work and went out for beer. We were proud and confident. —They sent our jobs to Mexico so Silicon Valley billionaires could make a buck. The Democrats and Republicans before Trump, none of them cared. But Trump …"

Sarah Lamb reached across and touched my wrist. "I'm

sorry." Her voice was really sweet then. "Donald does wonders, but he can only do so much. He created thousands of jobs in the oil industry by discovering something called *fracking*."

I felt a tear run down my cheek. I hadn't talked that way about losing my job to anyone. Those auto-workers had been my best friends ever, outside of Stan. I didn't want to wallow in it now, not lying on my back in the bottom of a well with some religious looney. Still, I said, "Trump's the only one who fights for guys like me. He tried to get GM to open up again."

She moved to my tarp and sat, looking down at me. She touched my thigh.

Yikes! I'd checked her out pretty well earlier—that wrinkled skin, at least sixty. Her body odor was no pleasure either, but her hand began to feel good, after I got used to it. I wanted to tell her.

"After that, I had nothing but crap jobs. Pumping gas, driving a limo for rich pricks—rich men. When I got laid off, my brother-in-law took me on as an investigator, damned pity job."

She patted my leg. "Is this all right, Bud? Touching is a lovely human connection."

"Sure." As long as that was all she wanted.

"You've had a hard time. Crying heals. I'll pray with you. That will help."

I had no use for that, but this woman, crazy or not; her soothing voice touched me, that and her warm hand.

NOVEMBER 5

HOW IN HELL was I going to make it all the way up there with only empty containers for steps?

Don't let yourself think that way, I told myself. *You have not one damned thing to lose.*

My three cans from the night before were still solid. I replaced the fourth and pounded in more tins, two by two, up to eye level. Keeping close against the wall, I stepped onto the first two cans. They held. The second pair held too. I managed to balance on them and wedge another can in above the others. I struck it with the bean can. I lost my balance and fell, but the cans didn't. I got up and tried again, climbing three feet above the floor. Balancing there, afraid to breathe, Sarah handed me another empty can, and another. I couldn't believe I'd gotten so far.

Five feet above the ground, I was just beginning to wonder if we had enough cans to make it all the way to the top, when the two I was standing on gave a little. I clawed at the wall to hold on, but all I got were handfuls of sandy crud. I tumbled in an avalanche of dirt, rock and empty tin cans. The fall knocked the wind out of me. My chest and legs were covered pretty deep, but it felt more like a heavy blanket of sand than a ton of concrete. I lay there, gasping, as Sarah scooped dirt away with her hands.

"It's okay, Bud. I'll get you out."

When she was half done, I flexed my legs and arms and pulled them free. I was okay. I rested there, looking up at the void I'd created. It ran all the way up, threatening to undermine one of the supports for the metal framework at the top. If that went down, there'd be one hell of a cave-in. Might kill us, would definitely make the framework useless. Jake/Jeff wouldn't be able to send down supplies, or hoist me and Sarah out. The longer I gazed up, the narrower the shaft became, the more trapped I felt. I closed my eyes and tried to devise a plan that didn't involve bringing the whole friggin' world crashing down.

CHAPTER 44

STAN

November 7-8

When did I stop thinking of Hannah as a damsel in distress and start seeing her as the girl who'd ditched me our freshman year of college? –the woman wanting my help to dispense with her husband? When had I stopped pursuing Jake Christian for my former sweetheart and decided to solve the case to prove that we could? We *would* solve it, but Bud came first. I didn't have energy for both.

Melanie entered my room that next morning wearing blue jeans and a black tee shirt with a silver Oakland Raiders logo. She set a cup of coffee on the night stand. "My sister delivered the motorhome this morning, while you slept. We can load up when you're ready."

I sipped the coffee and then texted Hannah to say that I was going to New Mexico following a lead in her husband's case.

Next, I called the Gallup Police Department, the McKinley County NM Sheriff and NM State Police to report Bud missing—over seventy-two hours now, so they had to pay attention. They entered information into their records. —I heard their computer keys clacking over the phone.

I dressed and threw a few things in a bag, then followed Mel out to see the olive-and-beige motorhome, sitting at the curb outside my house. It was on the small side, with a pickup truck cab and the living space running behind and over top. What really got my attention was the smashed-in front fender and the rusty scrape that ran from entry door to back bumper.

"You knew about this?" I pointed at the fender.

"My sister emailed pictures, before she picked it up." Melanie grinned at me. "We saved you a ton of money renting this. Not only that, if I crash into a tree, they won't know the difference."

Inside was a little dinette area and a boxed-in bathroom, a sofa, a mini-kitchen. A bunk bed occupied a niche over the truck cab. A ladder behind the passenger seat ran up to it.

Mel watched me inspect everything. "In case you're thinking of turning this in on another model, this was the only one left to rent. Every American who can't fly on vacation is out in one of these."

Melanie made the sofa into a bed for me. She loaded our clothing and supplies. She took the wheel as I slept in back. We made it to Kingman AZ that night and ate Wendy's burgers. She parked behind a truck stop.

I hadn't thought much about sleeping arrangements, but now I eyed the bunk bed over the cab. "I'd offer to sleep there, but that ladder looks *really* steep."

"I got it. No way you're climbing up."

I put on PJs in the bathroom, came out and got into bed. Mel changed in there after me, and I watched her climb to the cramped space, her pajamas silky in the reflected light from the truck stop. She looked down at me and said, "No problem, I like sleeping folded like a jack knife."

"If you change your mind, the bed's a queen." I couldn't believe I'd had the nerve for that.

In the night, I got up to go to the bathroom. In the dim light, I saw her watching from up there. "Can't sleep?"

"This isn't working," she said. "I tried to turn on my other side and almost got stuck. I'll be too tired to drive in the morning."

"Come on down."

I turned on my side, facing the wall. The mattress shuddered, as she climbed in. It felt awkward. She'd flirted with me, and she was really attractive. I wondered if she was lying, like me, timidly turned away. I wanted to shift onto my back to get more comfortable. Instead, I stayed cramped on a narrow slice of mattress.

What would it be like if Hannah was there instead? Married Hannah, sexy and brash, demanding that we strip down for lovemaking. I wasn't sure I wanted that, wasn't sure I trusted her. —I absolutely didn't.

Gradually, my tension let up. Mel wasn't demanding or devious. She'd come to help me find Bud. I eased onto my back and let myself breathe. Her presence began to feel like a warm breeze filling my sails.

I woke early the next morning, feeling a little better. I slipped out of bed. When Mel went to the bathroom, I set out cereal, milk, and bowls. She joined me at the dinette, looked me in the eye and asked, "Ever think you'd be sleeping with a black woman?"

I took a moment, and she added, "Just say it out straight, the way you feel it."

"You're a woman that's all," I said.

"Keep talking."

I didn't know what to say. "I always thought—since high school anyway—that America would be better if there were more mixed-race couples." I blushed, thinking, but not saying, *Not that we're a couple.*

"Armchair liberal," she said.

I took a few breaths, wondering what to say. "It sounds hokey, I know. I'm trying to be honest. I didn't get to know any black girls in school."

She poured milk into her cereal and chuckled. "You got to know white-as-snow Hannah."

Wondering how much Bud had told her, I said, "White as snow, sure."

"Feel different in bed with me?"

"I never made it to bed with Hannah."

She gave me the *eye.* "Mmm-hmm."

"Having you beside me felt nice. Okay, I was aware you're black, which made it different. But not so much. If you were Chinese or Swedish or Texan, I'd be aware of a difference."

She laughed, "Especially Texan."

"We're not in a relationship, and that made it a little strange."

"And you're my boss, sort of. Can I tell you something I shouldn't?"

"Sure."

"I liked sleeping beside you, Stan. I didn't want to get into that bunk in the first place. I hope you won't ask me to shinny up there again tonight."

I DROVE A LITTLE WHILE, and Mel finished the job. We ended up at a campground near Gallup. I took a shower. Mel followed and emerged from the bathroom, black hair, down to her shoulders, all wet and curly. I got up from the dinette where I'd been sitting.

Mel wrapped her arms around me. "We're both worried about him. We're in this together, Stan."

We held each other for maybe a minute. That made me feel better.

I was in bed first. The overhead light wasn't much, but I let myself enjoy the sight of Mel in those sleek PJs. She flipped off the light and sat on the side of the bed.

"You sure this is okay, Stan?"

"Jump in. The bed's warm." *Feeling brave.*

She joined me, pressing her forehead against my shoulder for a moment before moving to her side.

A couple of minutes later— "Still awake, Stan?"

"Yep."

"This doesn't mean anything, right? We're just two friends."

"We are, Mel. I really want that." I thought for a moment and said, "After we find Bud, we may need to go to Florida and track down Sarah Lamb."

"We?" Mel said.

"You and me."

"In this motorhome?"

"This is really nice, but I'm thinking airplane."

"After we test negative," she said.

"Right." If it wasn't for the comfort it gave me having her there, my worry for Bud might have kept me awake. More likely, Corona Virus would still have sent me to dreamland.

CHAPTER 45

BUD

NOVEMBER 7

I woke, sore as hell from sleeping on a tarp on pebbly dirt. There was a clunking sound from above. I looked up and saw a bearded face staring down—Jake/Jeff. He had a large metal basket suspended by rope from the pulley on the framework up there. Jake/Jeff lowered it down to us. More canned foods and chips, water, toilet paper, a couple of small propane bottles.

Thinking—*I could make one of these into a bomb and blast us out of this hole.* Not my best idea.

The basket came within reach, and I started tossing things out of it.

Jake/Jeff shouted down, "Don't try to get in the basket. I'll just drop the rope down on your head."

Yeah. Shit.

I removed the last water bottles and released it. It rose, and Jake/Jeff said, "I'll send down more blankets. It's getting cold."

"Damn right, it's cold," I shouted. "Why are you doing this?"

No answer.

"How long you gonna keep us here?"

"Not too long."

"Has Trump won yet?"

"In his dreams." Loud, bizarre laughter echoed in the shaft.

The basket came down again. I took the blankets and yelled, "My friend is going to find us, you son of a bitch."

When Jake/Jeff disappeared, I sat on one of the tarps with Sarah. She shook her head. "He delivers food every few days." She pouched her lips, and I thought she might cry again. "He'll let us go soon. He loves me."

I gave a snort. "A kid's love for his mother; that's the best kind."

"Where was my son living before?" she asked.

"Manhattan Beach, near LA. He was a cheesy con man selling fake statues and … stuff."

"But you came looking for Jeff."

"I told you I'm an investigator. His wife asked me and my partner, Stan, to find him."

Sarah perked up and stared at me. "What's her name, Jeff's wife? Do I have grand children?"

"Hannah's the wife. Your grandson's a college brat named Luke."

"Hannah … Hannah. What's she like?"

"She's cheesy too, a beautiful phony. You don't want me to say what she is."

I got up and paced, avoiding the latrine—four steps, turn, four steps. My body still ached from lying on the gravel, but moving helped. Sarah Lamb crab-walked back to the wall and sat, watching me.

After a while, Sarah said, "Jeff was special. When he was little, God gave us a sign. Do you believe in that, Bud—God communicating with people?"

"Not so much."

"It turned out piercing Jeff's hand was God's second sign, but I didn't recognize the first one right away. You know about Jeff's hands, don't you?"

"Sure." *Pretty damned weird.* "Just for fun, what was the first sign?"

"The Lord slew my husband, Byron. Byron was a good man, a salesman, but he discouraged me from my holy calling." She sighed. "He died in an accident in '86. I questioned God. I did, like you Bud, but God knew best."

Almost sensible compared to some of her shit. I heard the crunch of gravel, as Sarah shifted against the wall, but I didn't turn to look at her.

"Most people might have missed the point, but God was very methodical, unfettering me from my husband for holy purpose, then piercing one of Jeff's hands. Later the holy spirit burned Jeff's other hand with a bolt of lightning, right in the palm. Nothing could have been more obvious! We went off preaching the Lord's message after that. People flocked to us, and we saved them." Sarah gave a sorrowful sigh. "When Jeff left me, I was lost. I wandered in the wilderness, up on these mesas." She waved an arm toward the top of the shaft. "Just as our Lord wandered, until my dear second husband, Cedric, found me. His arrival was my fourth communication from God, a holy challenge. Cedric brought me to a new land and taught me new ways to look at the Divine. How privileged I am that God contacts me. And then …"

Here it comes; another friggin' sign.

"And then, my dear Cedric died in his sleep. I didn't question God this time. I knew He had plans for me."

I stood over her now catching a whiff of her BO. I moved a little further away and squatted on a tarp. "Having your ass dumped down in this hole with me; that's gotta be a sign of some kind. What's up with that?"

"You can be crude, Bud, but I sense you're a good man. My next sign involved Donald J. Trump and his holy mission."

"Amen," I said, and I broke out laughing.

CHAPTER 46

STAN

NOVEMBER 9-10, NEW MEXICO

We consulted the Highway Patrol and Gallup police. Bud hadn't checked out of his Comfort Suites east of Gallup, and he hadn't been seen in days. His bill was past due, his belongings moved to storage.

The state police had located Bud's blue Mustang by a dirt road in the forest south of Bluewater Lake. They'd sent a search crew out with dogs but found nothing. His car had been towed to an impound lot in Grants NM.

We weren't allowed into Bud's motel room, but the cops assured us there had been "no signs of mayhem." We headed to Grants to see Bud's car. My chest went hollow, as I climbed in. I'd ridden with Bud in that car dozens of times. This was real. My friend was in trouble. Aside from a thick covering of road dust, the Mustang yielded no clues. Except that there were no maps inside that vehicle. Bud was a map guy.

Back in Gallup, Mel hired a paralegal to check property records. According to the McKinley County Assessor's Office, Sarah Lamb still owned a parcel with a dwelling unit, east of

Crownpoint. The Assessor's maps broke the country into bits and pieces. The paralegal brought us eleven plat diagrams, covering hundreds of acres. When pieced together, they indicated the route from New Mexico 371 near Crownpoint to Sarah Lamb's isolated parcel. Mel cleared the dinette table and laid out a few land plats at a time. I traced the crooked lines, dirt roads, that branched one way and another from one paper onto another. Bud would have done this same thing almost a week back.

Mel drove us east and then north toward Crownpoint. After a few passes, we found the turnoff. Mel maneuvered the motorhome onto the dirt track that climbed toward a chalk-colored mesa. Dusty. Bumpy. We passed grazing sheep and came to an octagonal home made of plywood with a shingle roof, a *hogan*, as these Navajo dwellings were called. Nearby was a pen made of wooden branches holding two brown-and-white horses. A few Native American kids came from behind the building to gawk.

A red pickup truck barreled up, precipitating a dust cloud. The truck bounced past our motorhome and blocked us in. I saw a shotgun on its rack in the back window. Two Navajo men in black cowboy hats jumped out and stood by their truck. Mel looked nervous, as I felt. We put on masks and got out.

The two men, dark skin, maybe fifty and thirty—father and son?—glared at us. We all kept our distances. The father said something in Navajo, and the son translated. "You *Bilagáanas* think we're a tourist attraction?"

"No," I said. "We're looking for someone."

"My father wants you to leave."

I swallowed and took a breath. "My friend; he's missing. We think he came here." My voice cracked as I said it.

The father pointed at his chest and spoke Navajo. Translation from the son— "Your friend is one of us?"

"An Anglo," I said. "Is that the right word?"

"My father has a reason to resent tourists. Even out here you come, a few each year, taking pictures to bring back home. Mesas and cute Navajo kids. Backward. Quaint." The son glanced at the children and then gestured up the road toward the mesa. "Our people live in all these homes, except the last one."

"You know who lives there?" Melanie asked.

The son took off his hat and mopped his brow with his sleeve. "It was deserted for years. Then a man moved in last month. Has a beard. Drives a green Bronco. Doesn't stop to chat."

"Has he had visitors?" Mel asked.

"One car. In and out."

"A Mustang?"

The son looked at the father. "Blue, that's all I saw."

The color of Bud's car.

"Your father speaks English," I said, watching the older man to confirm.

The father turned and reached into their pickup. I heard a clack, as he unlatched the shotgun from the back window.

"He went to Crownpoint High School, like I did," the son said. "He played basketball for the Eagles. He likes you *Bilagáanas* okay, just not up here where we live." The son eyed our motorhome. "You won't get up there in that, not even close. I doubt the little blue car made it all the way." He looked me over. "The up-hill walk is a bitch."

He had a point. I was pretty well done for.

The father stood beside his truck, shotgun cradled in his arms, as we retreated, making plans to rent a pickup truck and try again.

CHAPTER 47

JEFF

NOVEMBER 5-8

After he deposited Bud Randolph in the pit, Jeff checked the guy out on the internet—real name, Andrew, military service in Iraq, employed at S. Stein Investigations. No wonder the guy had found Jeff; he was a god-damned private eye!

When Jeff brought provisions for his captives, two days later, Bud Randolph shouted from the bottom of the pit, "My friend is going to find us, you son of a bitch."

Randolph's warning bounced around inside Jeff's cranium. The guy was a *detective*. His friend must be *S. Stein Investigations*! The buzzing filled his head so full that it jiggled his ear lobes. His fears repeated over and over. He couldn't sleep. Ruby jumped off the bed, turned into that mummified ghost, and settled on the floor, covering her ears with her paws. Finally, he nodded off, waking around 10 AM. Both hands trembling now. Buzzing, constricting confusion. All he could think was, *Escape!*

Jeff grabbed his clothing and tossed it into the Bronco. He loaded lots of canned food, propane, and water and headed for Benny Begay's place. He'd lower supplies down to his *guests*, enough to hold them for a week, while he came up with a plan. Ruby sat beside the driveway, furred in her beautiful brown and white. She glanced at him, sorrowful. *Please don't leave me.* She turned her back. He opened the Bronco's door and called her, but she ignored him. Tears ran down his cheeks, as he pulled away. He looked in the sideview mirror, catching a last glimpse.

He reached Benny Begay's house. Damn it; Benny was gone! The truck, and its winch, gone—no way to safely provide food to them. Jeff's head buzzed louder, like it had that last time onstage with his mother. He'd passed out after that. That would be a disaster if it happened now.

He fought the dizzies and sped all the way to Flagstaff, four hours of close calls with big rig trucks and roadside ditches, before stopping. He bought a pint of gin and a bottle of tonic. He parked in a sparse neighborhood, surrounded by pine tries and opened a can of Spam, Teriyaki Flavor. He alternated forkfuls with shots of gin and gulps of tonic. Halfway through the liquor, he thought about how little water they had down in that pit. His mother was a menace, but Bud Randolph didn't deserve to die! He scribbled a note to Benny explaining where to find the old mine shaft.

It's really important, Benny. Please go right away.

He slept in the truck. Next morning, Jeff headed south. The letter went east by US Mail Priority Express, to Benny Begay, General Delivery, Crownpoint NM.

CHAPTER 48

STAN

Mel and I returned to the campground near Gallup. We laid in provisions and rented a pickup truck.

I called Sergeant Lopez at the McKinley County Sheriff and explained the situation.

"Not my jurisdiction," he said. "Contact the Navajo Nation Police in Crownpoint." He hung up before I could ask more questions.

That next morning, we drove the dirt roads, following the plat maps to the plain wood cabin, a short walk past the end of the dirt road. No vehicles there. The door was locked, shutters closed tight, except one in the back that had fallen off, window latch broken. Mel climbed through and let me in. Inside we found a shelf with a few canned goods, an old armchair and a couple of beds. There was a desk with a photo of Sarah and Jeff Lamb in their preaching outfits, a picture of Jesus on the shelf, and lots of Christian books. We'd found their hide away, but there were no other personal possessions, none of Jake Christian's clothing!

Mel and I canvassed the Navajo homes along the dirt roads near the cabin. The people were wary at first. *Indian tourism* was unwelcome, and Covid-19 was rampant in Navajo country. We kept our distance and explained our mission. They'd all seen Jake Christian's green Bronco. A couple remembered the blue Mustang that had come and gone, but that was all.

At a *hogan*, just down the hill from Jake's cabin, a middle aged Native American named Benny Begay knew more. Benny checked out our picture of Jake Christian and confirmed his identity; except Hannah's husband had grown a beard and called himself Jeff. Benny had talked with him several times. Their mothers had known each other years before, and Benny had loaned Jake his pickup truck. Jake's green Bronco had been gone for about a day.

I worried more than I wanted to admit, more than I wanted Mel to see. When we got back to the motorhome that afternoon, she gave me hugs and reassurance. I told her I needed a little alone time and went to sit outside.

After a half hour of unproductive worry, I cleared my mind enough to think about the case. If Jacob Christian didn't turn up here in New Mexico, we had that other lead. I pulled out my cell and called the Lord's Chapel in Florida, expecting to reach an answering machine. Instead, the church secretary answered with a southern drawl. She confirmed that Sarah Lamb was still missing. I asked if Sarah had contacted them or left any word before leaving. "She didn't tell us one solitary thing," the woman said. "Maybe she got the Corona." She didn't laugh, but I got the feeling she wanted to.

The woman gave me her name and said it would be okay to check in with her again. If we didn't find Jake here in New Mexico, Florida would be next. But not before we found Bud.

EACH DAY WE STOPPED by the cabin. We checked in with local agencies. We had flyers printed with Bud's picture and provided them to the police and businesses in Crownpoint. We stood outside the supermarket or the Crownpoint Health Care Facility holding Bud's picture.

"Have you seen this man? He was driving a blue Mustang."

No one recognized him. I wanted to pound my fist on the dashboard on the way back to our campground late each day.

My symptoms were going away. Mel was doing fine. Getting past Covid! We went for tests at a drive-through site at Walgreens in Gallup, results due in three days.

Each evening, Mel or I cooked on the propane burners—hamburgers, omelets, canned chili. We ordered pizza delivery. I couldn't concentrate to read, so Mel and I downloaded comedies from Netflix. We watched on my laptop at the dining table until I was ready to drop.

In bed, Mel's right hand and my left hand met in the no man's land at the center, saying without words what I needed: *It's okay. I'm here for you.* Then we each turned away to sleep.

The fourth day at the campground, as sunrise sent first light through the windows, Mel moved close behind me and wrapped her arm around my chest. I can't express how good it felt.

No man's land had been breached. Some comfort given. Affection growing.

CHAPTER 49

BUD

November 12

Another day, another night, and another, and … Quiet most of the time. No way to climb out or blast our way out. I considered digging—slowly collapsing one side of the pit to make a ramp. *Collapsing* scared the shit out of me. *Collapsing* meant bringing that metal hoist thing crashing down.

It was dark that night, with just the glow from the heater. Sarah Lamb and I lay on our separate tarps. I could make out a few stars and the shape of the framework up there. I heard her breathing nearby. I sat up.

"Can't sleep?" Sarah asked.

"How could a guy, lying on this gravelly crap?"

"I've asked you not to swear," she said.

"*Crap* is me cleaning up the word *shit*."

She let out an exasperated sigh.

We hadn't eaten since canned beans and potato chips at high noon. My stomach screamed for food. Corn, tuna, Cheetos; they'd run out the day before. Now we had only the last two *delicacies*. Sarah's son hadn't shown up to deliver supplies in five days.

Maybe I'd scared Jake/Jeff off by saying my friend would come. Maybe the heater's propane would run out and hypothermia would take us down. I'd read on the internet how a couple of nuns, stuck in an elevator somewhere, had saved their lives by drinking urine—fake news or life-saving factoid? Anyway, I'd begun pissing in empty bottles. My piss wasn't real dark. If I had to drink it, I would, but there were still a couple of fresh bottles. I'd confiscated them when Sarah prepared to use one for a sponge bath.

Seven days in this pit, eight? Sarah launched into little homilies from time to time. She was a preacher after all. Mostly I ignored the words, but her tone soothed me. She was a human presence, female, melodic most of the time. She told me a little about her life between random biblical messages. Now she was talking about one of her dead husbands again. Byron or Cedric? I wasn't sure.

Sarah's voice quavered. Couldn't blame her for crying, trapped in this tomb. My stomach told me to goddamn open the last can of Spam. I sat up and tried the flashlight—feeble, but some help.

"Time to gobble it down, Sarah."

"We agreed to save it for breakfast."

"Can't do it."

"You can, Bud. Don't think about your hunger. Tell me something interesting about those workers' comp cases you investigate."

The only interesting thing was that Sarah Lamb had asked. Still, it was a chance to challenge her sanctimonious BS. I flicked off the light to conserve. "Well, Sarah, one of our suspects claimed a debilitating mental defect from his time as a postal worker. Who would have thought sorting packages at three AM would drive a guy nuts?"

Sarah sat upright on her tarp, the dim light of the heater gleaming on her blond hair. I had her attention.

"I questioned the guy and his wife, and they both told the same story. With him working nights they didn't see each other much, so they began an *open marriage*. You ever hear of that?" I paused to see if she'd answer, and also to think up a better story. "The wife ordered their condoms from a big drugstore chain, but they only used two dozen in ten years." I saw Sarah studying me, which made me foolishly happy. "Not that they didn't have plenty of partners," I said. "She bought one dozen blue and one dozen pink rubbers. They rinsed them out each time and used them over. He got the blue, and she got the pink. Or was it the other way around?" I laughed at my own inventiveness.

"You mustn't make a joke of sin." Her eyes shone in the darkness. Outraged? Her voice didn't sound that way. "You're a scamp, aren't you, Bud?"

"True story, Sarah."

"Jamaica," she said. "That's where I lived the last nineteen years with my Cedric."

"The news said Indonesia."

"You believe the fake news? Hasn't Donald taught you anything?"

"But why?"

"I might have mentioned Indonesia to a couple of reporters." She gave what I took for a sly smile. Hard to tell with just the light from the heater. "I told you about my beautiful Cedric. He was a Rastafarian, the most enchanting people God ever created, so simple and open. They adore me."

She winked at me; I was pretty sure.

"Cedric was the most passionate man. His people are devoted to Jesus and other prophets."

"Smoke much dope there?" I asked.

"Ganja, Bud. Medicinal and mind expanding. My life was idyllic."

"And you left, because?"

"Because of Donald, of course. He came to me in a vision, over the internet. I'd always kept up with the news, but after Cedric died, I went to town every day and used the library's computer."

"When you set your ganja pipe down and came up for air," I offered.

"I saw Donald on the screen, almost as beautiful as my Cedric."

Trump beautiful? Maybe women saw him differently.

"Donald mocked the pompous do-gooders. He denounced the godless ones who excused abominations. Pornographers! Homosexuals! Rapists! Illegals! Donald called them out. But Donald was a scamp with the women. I questioned how such a lustful man could achieve righteous ends. Still, week after week, America's evangelicals flocked to him. He won the election and appointed God's chosen judges to the High Court. Donald encouraged Israel to annex more and more. The Biblical Land ascending! When Christ returns, He will behold what Donald Trump has wrought, and He will smile!"

Sarah was sitting very straight on the tarp, passionate. "But there were twin plagues! Our Donald was challenged by a made-up disease called Corona. An election was coming. His enemies closed in like jackals, wanting to steal the vote. Now was not the time for His people to stand aside. Now was the time to march with God and Donald Trump."

"So you hustled your ass back to America and began preaching again."

She leaned toward me and touched my forearm. "I'll tell you a secret, Bud, if you promise not to mention it to my son."

"I don't plan to speak to your son."

"My secret is: sometimes, Bud, just sometimes, a little crudeness excites me."

Flirting? Jesus!

"What I plan to do with your son is cram that can of Spam up his rectum."

"You minimized the crudeness. I appreciate that."

"But first you and I will empty it." With the crappy light from the dying flashlight and the heater, I forked the remaining Spam and the last of the pinto beans onto our filthy plates—Sarah's yellow plate, mine green—making me think, that the condoms in my story should have been yellow and green. I sat against the wall, and she joined me a couple of feet away. I handed Sarah her share.

She brought the plate up near her face. "This doesn't smell so awful."

"Too bad it's not Jalapeño."

I switched off the flashlight, but I could make out the glint of her fork moving.

"You made that up, didn't you?" she said. "The condoms."

"I thought you'd enjoy it." I finished eating, lapped my plate like a dog, and set it down.

She spoke softly. "My son may not come back."

"I thought of that."

"We could die here." She shifted. I felt her close by.

I thought of asking how divine her precious Jeffy seemed right now. "Yeah."

"You should have let me clean myself. Jesus likes women to be pure when they pray."

I considered offering her a bottle of piss. "He'll forgive you this time."

"He always does. That's the thing, Bud. Will you pray with me?"

"You start. Don't wait up for me." I saw something that might have been a smile in the darkness.

"You support President Trump, so you must believe that God sent Donald to us."

"Trump *is* here to save America, but his angel wings fell off on a deep dive down under."

"America." She took in another loud breath. "America, God shed His grace on thee. Don't you see? Donald cannot be separated from the love of Jesus."

I had to laugh, remembering that video of Trump bragging about fingering women's nether parts.

Sarah moved still closer and touched my hand.

How goddamned fascinating these days in this well had been. To be drugged and wake up with a famous evangelist, a nutty one raving about Jesus and Trump in the same sentence. The story of this moment sounded fake, but I could sell it to one of those inquiring magazines. People who read those rags had open minds, open enough to believe anything, messianic imaginings all the better. And this tale would be true. The way she held my hand now felt tender, her voice comforting.

"You seem happy, Bud."

"My stomach's full of Spam, and I'm thinking that while we're trapped here, Trump's fighting like hell. When we get out, he'll be president again."

"Yes, Bud. Yes."

"I can feel it."

"Defeating the Godless liberals, sending illegals back to where they belong."

Sarah Lamb moved so her thigh pressed against mine, one of her breasts against my arm. She cupped my cheek in her hand and kissed me full on the mouth.

CHAPTER 50

NOVEMBER 12, 13

Sarah had been a beautiful woman. I knew that from her pictures on the internet. Now she was old—sixties anyway. Her face was—what was the term? —*etched deep*, with gullies from years of sun worship. Lots of sun in Jamaica. With her blond hair, it wasn't the worst look, if a woman had to turn friggin' sixty. She leaned into me.

It wasn't that she was old or ugly; she wasn't, exactly. It wasn't the rocks digging into my ass or the sand grinding my scrotum inside my jockey shorts. It was the smell. The ever-present stench of our waste filled the air, though I barely noticed anymore. Mostly, it was her breath, full of three-week-old Spam, that hadn't been brushed away, because her son hadn't bothered to provide toothpaste or brushes. Her BO reminded me of road kill. My stink had to be just as bad. Not exactly a romantic encounter.

I didn't think of any of that right then. When her lips attacked me, I shoved her hard. She landed a few feet away in the middle of the pit and yelped.

"Thanks, Sarah, but no," I said.

"We're going to die," she gasped.

"So, you're looking for one last fling?"

She cackled and crawled onto her tarp. I lay back down too, thinking about the story I could tell some rag of a magazine. This little episode I'd call, *the kiss of the vampire prophet*. Unless, of course, my story decayed with my rotting carcass in that pit.

THE MORNING AFTER my close encounter with Sarah, I woke to the sound of an engine up above. A strange face peered down at us—Native American.

"*Hello down there*," the man called.

"*Hey*," I shouted. "*Can you get us out of here?*"

The man lowered that large metal basket on a rope. I steadied Sarah, as she climbed in.

She gave me a wry smile. "We could go up together."

"I'll wait for the next gondola, thanks."

The fellow winched her up and lowered it back for me. When I reached the surface, the light was too damned bright. I closed my eyes and dropped to the ground.

The Native American guy stood, looking down at me. "You alright?"

I squinted at him. "Thanks, man. You've saved us. Are you Navajo?"

"Yeah. Benny Begay. I got a note from my neighbor, Jeff, to bring my truck with the winch and look into this old mine."

"Good old Jeff," I said.

I heard Sarah murmuring and looked over to see her kneeling on the ground. Giving thanks to her god most likely.

I shifted my stiff shoulders and stood up. I lifted my right foot, then my left, did a couple of knee bends and sat my ass back on the dirt. "What happened to Jeff?"

"People came nosing around his cabin. Guess it made him nervous. He took off a few days back."

"Tell me Benny; Trump won, right?"

"Not yet, but he's invited all you *Bilagáanas* to a big rally in Washington."

CHAPTER 51

STAN

November 13

My last call to Sergeant Lopez at the McKinley County Sheriff's Department went like all the others. No bodies had been found in County jurisdiction. Lopez referred me again to the Navajo Nation Tribal Police.

I was about to call them, when my phone chirped with a text from a strange number: *What's up, Stan? I called the office and got the answering machine—Bud.*

"Mel, look!" I showed her the screen and then texted him back: *Where the heck are you?*

My phone rang a few seconds later, and I answered.

"I'm in Gallup. A really great Navajo guy drove me and my new friend, Sarah, here."

Every muscle in my body relaxed at the sound of his voice. My heart drummed a joyful beat. "Happy coincidence, Bud. We're in Gallup too." Mel reached for my phone, and I handed it over.

"Bud, it's Melanie. Are you okay?" She laughed at something he said and gave the phone back to me.

"How long you been in Gallup?" Bud asked.

"A few days. I came down with Covid and it slowed us down."

He chuckled. "Funny, ain't it, all those times you made *me* mask up."

"Sure. Where have you been, pal?"

"Down a well."

Presumably that was a joke.

WE MET BUD a half hour later at a picnic table outside the Comfort Inn. I gave him the three Big Macs and giant Coke we'd bought for him.

He unwrapped a burger, took a big bite, chewed for a second, and swallowed. "How'd you get here?"

I pointed to our vehicle, parked across the lot, smashed fender and rusty gouges obvious in the mid-day sunlight. "See that motorhome?"

"Great fender art," Bud said. He scratched his head, pretending to think about something. "You're sleeping in there?" He rubbed his chin, glancing at Melanie. "Together?"

"Friends on the road," Mel said. "Cozy."

Between gulps of burger, Bud gave us a quick rendition of his adventures with Jake and Sarah Lamb, "the fucking amazing evangelist." He finished with, "Now my friends, you'll excuse me. I haven't slept worth shit in a week, and I'm heading home tomorrow." He scrunched his hamburger wrappers into a ball and shoved it into the bag. "Oh yeah, do you happen to know where my car is?"

Mel pointed toward the east. "In Grants, sixty miles that way."

CHAPTER 52

Mel and I hugged in bed that night. We caressed each other's backs. We kissed cheeks. The next morning, we slept in until 9.

"I feel okay, Mel. I'd like to drive."

I slid behind the wheel, and she joined me in the cab.

"Where do you want to go?" She gave me an innocent look, as if her question hadn't just turned things on their head.

I released the key without turning it. "Somewhere besides home?"

"My sister is looking after Mom." She enticed me with playful eyes. "There are amazing sights between here and LA. National Parks, scenic vistas …"

We had informed my clients; a couple of insurance companies and a state agency, about my medical situation. They'd work around my absence.

"We could squeeze in a few days," I said.

"I've been to the Grand Canyon. How about Utah?"

I imagined red rocks and natural arches. I imagined Mel and me together without the constant worry about Bud. I could still feel her holding me in bed the night before. "Sounds great."

"Monument Valley, I love the pictures from there."

"We may still be contagious. You all right sleeping in this buggy?"

She brandished a finger at me. "First we go to a laundromat, either that or burn the sheets and buy new."

While our laundry spun in the machines, we drank coffee at the motorhome dinette table. I sent Bud a text: *Hold down the fort, old friend. I'll be back in a week or so.* I sent a second text to Hannah. *Bud found your husband, but he's taken off again. I'm turning off my phone, so you should call him for the details.*

We gloved up and masked up, finished our laundry, and wiped everything with disinfectant.

Back in the motorhome, she looked more thoughtful. "Sure you're okay going on the road with me?"

"What do you mean, Mel? It sounds like fun."

"Me black, you white."

"I think we make a pretty fine *couple*." Can't believe I had the courage for that word.

"Not everyone would agree." She gestured toward the laundromat.

"Yeah, that scrawny old woman did give us the evil eye. Just ignore it." Truth was, I'd felt a little uncomfortable with her staring at us.

"Not too long ago, they'd have offered me a sink of dirty water out back for the 'colored folk.' Lots of them still don't want people like me soiling their machines. Or *couples* like us. Especially couples."

I watched her, the fingers of her left hand kneading her thigh, not angry so much as disgusted.

"I know, Mel. You're gorgeous and smart, and they're fools. I want very much to spend this time with you."

She smacked the dashboard with an open hand. "Cops killed George Floyd. Their hatred showed up on TV. You saw it. Every liberal white person saw it. Don't ask me to ignore it, okay? We've pretended to do that forever." She was looking straight ahead, but it felt like she was attacking me.

"Of course. I didn't ask that."

"If you're going with me to be politically correct, to show off something—"

"No, Mel! You're a special woman. Period. Black, sure. Beautiful, yes. Smart. A good companion." What I didn't say was, *I think I'm falling for you.* "Still want to travel with me?"

"I do." She gave me a weak smile, reached over and touched my hand. "You're not the kind of man to hate anyone."

We called in an order at a nearby grocery, food and celebratory wine. A young woman, wearing a mask and a white apron, delivered the goods.

I felt good, mostly healthy, driving in this open country, Mel on the passenger side taking in the sights. I was in control. I guess that's a *guy thing.* After a while that huge rock formation, Shiprock, loomed. We traveled miles before coming abreast of it. It disappeared behind us. We entered the town named for the rock.

"I made it two hours behind the wheel."

"Great job," Mel said, "What do you think of staying around here?" She wore a royal blue, long sleeve tee shirt that looked great on her, and she seemed altogether happy now.

"At this rate, we'll reach California sometime in spring," I said.

"We'll make up for it tomorrow; three hours on the road, for sure."

A little river flowed through town, the San Juan. I followed a one-lane road along its banks. The road climbed a hill and turned to dirt, and I pulled over. Mel and I got out and walked to a bluff above the river, running brown over rapids.

"I like the sound." She pointed to a ledge a few feet below us. "Want to sit for a while?" She didn't wait for an answer. "I'll get blankets and that bottle of rosé."

We sat on the blankets, sipping wine, and then, just naturally, lay down facing each other. The sun was low. We stared at one another like I'd never seen another woman or she another man, not someone so bewitching, anyway. *I love you, Mel*—one of those things I didn't say. I stroked my fingers over her face, her skin that lovely brown. In this light, shining directly on Mel, I saw her more clearly than before—no big glasses or mask, not the dim light of the motorhome, not a moment when I was too shy to study every feature. That unfamiliar quality I'd tried to identify in her face—her eyes, her cheekbones; not a movie star's, but somehow more pure. Not a "big-eyed girl," not closed off either. Desirable.

She beamed at me, and those eyes narrowed a little. "You're beautiful," she said.

I would have contradicted her, but she put fingers to my lips. She kissed my nose, my cheeks, my eyelids. I heard the gentle roar of the river below and the pulsing of my heart. Birds chirped nearby. She pressed her lips into my neck and ran her hand over my chest. "Feeling okay?"

"Feeling *wonderful*." I pulled her tight against me, staring at her face. Her eyelashes fascinated me. "May I?" I brought my left hand toward her right eye. She closed her eyes and I brushed my forefinger over the lashes. "Delicate," I said.

"Now yours." She grazed my lashes too. "I haven't felt this close to a man in a long time."

Later we settled in bed, and I reached for her hand. "What did that mean," I asked. "Holding each other that way?"

"I really like you." She pressed against me, her forehead to my cheek. She felt warm and luscious. Deep contentment settled in my chest. I wanted only to stay like that for a few minutes, an hour, all night.

"Mel, I want to kiss you."

"I thought you did." She waited.

"What's holding me back; it's not because I'm your almost-boss, or because I don't like you that way. It's the virus."

She rested a hand against my chest.

Illogical. We were in such close contact; any germs would leap from her to me. But I couldn't get over thoughts of Covid-19 swarming back and forth, lips to lips, tongue to tongue.

"Better to wait, Stan. When we're free of this, we'll be really free."

She rolled to her other side and I lay still, thinking. This was like Hannah and every other woman who'd come close to me; imagining possibilities that probably wouldn't pan out.

I slept and woke and felt her presence, the magic and fear of a new beginning. Did I want to leap off that cliff, hoping there were no rocks in the water below?

I wanted the sweetness of life. I wanted to splash in it.

Next morning, we received our Covid-19 results online. She tested clear. I didn't. I drove after breakfast. Mel sat silent for a few minutes and then looked at me.

"We shouldn't make too much of that amazing long hug on the ledge, right?"

"You mean when you stared into my eyes and the world disappeared around us?"

"Yeah, that hug."

I glanced at her and saw that she'd looked away.

"I have to admit, Stan. I've thought about you before."

I didn't know what to say.

"You're a nice guy in a sea of jerks. I find that attractive."

"You're the only gorgeous woman who's held me that way since …"

"This is a dangerous moment for us, Stan. You'd be smart to run like hell."

I thought a full minute about my answer, rehearsing it to myself, before saying aloud, "I only want to run toward you."

CHAPTER 53

We camped on Navajo land at Monument Valley, where desire overruled our Covid reluctance with a torrent of kisses. We stayed near Natural Bridges and Bryce Canyon and at a buffalo ranch close to Zion National Park. We didn't remove our PJs, but with buffalo grunting and munching grass just beyond the fence outside our motorhome, we explored not just natural wonders but human ones, sensual and tender.

In Las Vegas we drove through a Covid test site before heading home. I parked the motorhome at the curb outside my place, the vehicle confined to quarantine that week.

Mel and I took turns cooking. She could have slept in the guest room, but I invited and she accepted. We shared my bed.

Our results came back negative. We celebrated with sparkling wine and deep, amazing kisses. Mel had called her mother every day, and now that we were clear, I was afraid she'd head home the next day. But she said, "I have to be extra careful with her." We tested again, giving us another seventy-two hours.

That night, she came out of the bathroom wearing one of my dress shirts—turquoise. Her bare legs were long, supple, and enticing.

She let me admire her a moment before turning off the bedroom light. She climbed under the covers, and I ran my fingers along her thigh.

"Mel, you have great legs."

"I'm well covered," she said. "—In case you were wondering. I borrowed a pair of your underpants."

I savored the feel of her, as we kissed.

"I have a request," she said.

"I'm likely to accept."

"Do you think of me as one of the guys?"

"You, Mel, are all woman and nothing but."

"My name is Melanie."

"I'm sorry. You are *Melanie* and no one but."

She unbuttoned my pajama top. "Good. You'll find a gift in my pocket."

I ran my hand up to her breast, lingered there, slipped my fingers into the pocket that held a condom.

CHAPTER 54

Our tests came back negative again, and she spent the weekend at her mother's house.

At the office on Monday, she and I sipped our Starbucks and enjoyed a long reunion kiss before getting back to work.

Bud arrived around nine-thirty and scrutinized us. "Looks like *you've* been having fun. You got a little tan, Stan."

He focused on Melanie, as she strapped on her blue mask.

"Wow. You got contacts, Mel. And a new red dress? Stand up, so I can take a look. Jesus, you're hot." Bud looked from Melanie to me and back, as we glanced at each other. "And Stan's your boyfriend now?"

Bud turned his keen eyes on me. "You sure got over Hannah fast."

I felt myself blush. Melanie smirked at me, and I shook my head.

"I wasn't that into her," I said, realizing Hannah had vanished in my rear-view mirror without much thought. It really had been all about lust, hadn't it? Lust and a boyish fantasy. "You were right, Bud. She just wanted to use me."

"So you played the flash drive I made for you."

"Flash drive?" I vaguely remembered. "Oh, yeah. Melanie brought it the night I came down with Covid."

Bud groaned. "Come on, man. You didn't listen to it? I risked a lot placing that bug in Hannah's house."

"Bud! You broke in?"

He gave me a thumbs up. "You'll be glad. Wait till you hear that recording."

I should have been angry, but a secret recording of Hannah—that made me curious.

MELANIE AND I took off for an early lunch. We stopped to pick up Chinese takeout and went to my place. She divided the food onto plates, while I tracked down the flash drive and plugged it into my laptop. Mel picked up an egg roll, but she set it down when the recording started.

Hannah's voice—*Ralph, don't forget you're my lawyer.*

Man's voice, Ralph—*I'm more than that, honey.*

Hannah—*You are, totally, and you're going to get me a great divorce, either that or Jake's life insurance.*

Ralph—*Your private dick better find a body or make up some convincing shit. Make Jake look fucking dead; either that or video him in the hot tub with a gaggle of bimbos.*

Hannah—*I have a sweet spot for Stan. I really do, but he's slow to catch on. I invited him for a nude swim—*

Ralph—*Super idea.*

Hannah, laughing—*I got naked, and Stan started stripping. I mentioned Jake being dead, and his dick dangled. He pulled his clothes back on and made a run for my computer.*

Ralph, louder—*What's wrong with the guy? Focus him, Hannah. Tell him exactly what you need—dead or guilty as sin. Have him make stuff up if he has to. Get naked again, grab his dick and yank him into the pool with you. Pull him all the way down.*

Hannah—laughing again.

I stopped the playback, embarrassed and a little hurt.

Melanie was wide-eyed amazed. She picked up her egg roll and pretended to wring its neck. "If she grabbed you that way, would you dive in?"

I winced. "You want a serious answer?"

She took a bite of the dismembered egg roll, waiting.

"Hannah's really pretty, a great body, sexy eyes that draw a guy in." I watched her finish off her egg roll. "Then there's her phony neediness and shallow manipulation. That dream from twenty years ago intrigued me, but I've grown up."

Mel cut a pot sticker in half and speared it with her fork. "I'm not as attractive."

"That is *so* wrong. You're lovely. I love being with you. You cared for me when I was sick. You'd never trick me or use me."

"I'm trickier than you think."

I waited.

"Give me your third pot sticker and I'll show you."

CHAPTER 55

BUD

December 1, 2020 to January 5, 2021

Democrats were stealing the election. I knew that, but sometimes, falling off to sleep, I revved up my skeptical side. Votes could be stolen in either direction. One man's claim was another's fucking lie. What if the liar and the ly-ee were switched? I watched hours of Fox TV—Sean Hannity; I love that guy—and One America, bolstering my certainty by feeding on the truth.

Stan hadn't wanted to talk about it before. Now I didn't either. If we did, Stan would take Biden's side, even though he didn't like Biden that much, even though the steal was a travesty. Stan was gullible. He'd fallen for the party line, and it was the wrong party. Just like he'd fallen for that phony slut, Hannah. Hannah was just a beguiling piece of ass. This was not some petty disappointment; this was my truest friend. This was depressing.

Then my early morning, half-awake self whispered, *Donald's beguiling too.*

No. No. No. Watch the news. Watch One America News. Donald is the only one who'll tell the truth. Donald will bring back American jobs, the kind we gotta have.

STAN

JANUARY 1, 2021

GOOD THINGS were happening, but I couldn't savor them.

Joe Biden was about to become president. Trump would be gone. We'd solved our big case and liberated Bud. My friend was home and healthy, but he was bound for Washington in two days for the big Trump rally. I couldn't speak to the man who should have been my dear friend. I could barely look at him. This political duplicity had exposed the country I love, which was not the country I thought it was. There were people who would destroy democracy to get their way, not just a fringe group but half of the Republican Party, they said. My God, Bud was one of them. He believed that Trump won the election, despite a total lack of evidence! He didn't rule out anarchy!!!

I told myself, *Cling to the happiest note: Melanie.* She and I were working together and having lunch together, sleeping half of the nights wrapped in each other's arms. Yes!!!

CHAPTER 56

BUD

January 5, Nighttime, Washington, D.C.

Looking over the crowd, I saw the Capitol building to one side, the Washington monument the other way. Both lit by floodlights, awe-inspiring. The majesty of America's government, Donald Trump's government. Now the presidency was threatened. The people here—had to be over a thousand of us—wore quilted coats and bomber jackets, red MAGA hats. Trump banners and flags waived in the breeze. Every one of us righteously pissed.

It was Sarah's turn onstage. She wore a white robe and a long, blond wig. She raised her hands high and crooned her message to the people, as my attention drifted in and out.

"The evil ones try to steal our holy election. ... Satan lives! Satan infests our government and the souls of those who deny God. The ones who tear down statues and burn buildings ... We must have faith. We *can* defeat the god of darkness. ..."

I'd come to Washington to support the president, but also because of Sarah. In my head I was composing my article for that inquiring rag; me and Sarah kidnapped, down a well, rescued by a Navajo. Fantastic story! Sarah in Washington for a miracle, the rescue of America's presidency. I was witness to all of it. Trump would probably invite me to the White House after the article came out.

Jesus wasn't a deal for me, but somehow, contrary to good sense, in my heart, I saw something holy in Sarah. In that white robe with the lights on her, she had … an aura.

Stop it! You don't believe in holy or heart or aura.

The people cheered. Sarah stepped down from the podium. A black guy in a camouflage jacket stuck a microphone in front of her. A big woman in a black coat steadied a TV camera on her shoulder and flooded Sarah with light.

"Ms. Lamb," the guy said. "Jordan Yazz from Channel Ten. You left your ministry in Florida back in October. There's a rumor you went to meet your son, Jeff."

Sarah gave a toothy smile. "I'm *Reverend* Lamb. Will this be a scoop for you?"

"You and Jeff are a fascinating story. Our viewers would love to know."

"My son and I had a lovely visit," she said.

My mind flashed to Jake/Jeff lowering Spam down in a basket.

"Where is Jeff?" the reporter asked. "Does he plan to join your ministry?"

A cold breeze blew Sarah's blond hair into her eyes. She brushed it back. "Are you a religious man, Jordan? Do you know about Jesus's time in the wilderness? There were no reporters then. If there had been, they wouldn't have found our Lord until he wanted to be found."

"You're comparing your son, Jeff Lamb, to Christ the Lord. Is that correct, Reverend Lamb?"

"My son is blessed by the Holy Hand. He will reenter his ministry when God wishes it. Now please turn that off." She pointed at the camera woman with her light. "My boyfriend and I are returning to our motel now."

Fuck! If anything could have made me puke right then, the thought of being Sarah Lamb's boyfriend would be it.

The spotlight turned on me, as Sarah took my arm. I ducked and pulled her away through the scattering crowd.

CHAPTER 57

JANUARY 6, 2021

Sarah and I slept in adjacent rooms at a motel in Virginia. To be clear, I accompanied her because of the story for the tabloids and NO OTHER REASON. The next morning, we took a cab across the Potomac, dropping us as near to the White House as possible. We followed the patriotic warriors, Trump banners and US flags waving, signs bobbing, a few yellow *Don't Tread on Me* flags, too. Young women handed us red MAGA hats, and we put them on, as we passed through metal detectors and arrived at the back of the crowd. No one wore a mask in that sea of red hats.

On a stage, protected by plexiglass, with the White House behind, speakers led chants of *Stop the Steal, Make America Great Again. Lock her up.* Why the hell did they still care about Hillary? Rudy Giuliani gave a speech, which didn't inspire me. Giuliani, like Sarah's Satan nonsense, was a little too far off track.

The president stepped onstage. A dozen of the flags he loved waved behind him. I felt an awe I'd never experienced. (*Awe*— not part of my normal vocabulary.) Sarah stood on tiptoes beside me, radiant. I heard no sound but the president's voice for those amazing minutes. Absorbing, accepting, as Trump declared it: The election had been stolen. I believed it more at that moment than

I had at any time, even binge-watching Fox. Trump's confident voice declared, "We're going to walk down. ...I'll be there with you. ... Walk down to the Capitol."

The president left the stage. As Sarah and I followed the crowd, I kept watching for a black limousine flying small American flags from the fenders, but I knew, didn't I? Trump wasn't coming. And if he wasn't ...

My nagging cynicism whispered, *If one party can steal votes, the other can too.*

Beguiling. The word popped back into my head. I wanted to spit it out.

Trump will always do the right thing. —That's what I'd told myself.

A man shouted, "Hang Mike Pence." I saw a few guys in red caps carrying a fake gallows with a noose dangling. Mean looking dudes. Not the kind you'd hang out with.

I stepped aside, letting them all go by. Trying to catch a glimpse through the swell of banners and flags, I saw part of the crowd surge up the Capitol steps. I heard war whoops and a pounding up ahead.

"We're gonna git em," a guy shouted. "We're comin' right behind ya."

"What are you waiting for?" Sarah asked.

"I don't know."

A woman nearby, her hair red as blood, looked up from her cell phone and called out, "They've broken in. Fuck that shit-head Biden. They're in!"

I thought, *That wild babe would vote twice for Trump, if she had the chance—five times. So would those guys with the gallows.*

And then, *They're invading our sacred building.*

Sarah's eyes shone, like they had on stage the night before. "Look at them, Bud. The truth is with us. Truth is what the people believe."

Truth? I thought. *What the fuck is that?*

CHAPTER 58

STAN

Mid-January 2021

Jacob Christian was missing again, maybe down in Mexico. That was Bud's guess. Bud and I liked to speculate about that and about how he'd managed to slip drugs into Bud's can of iced tea. We hashed over lots of stuff.

Joe Biden was heading to the White House. Bud refused to discuss it, not even a casual mention. My old army buddy did talk up one thing, though: last week's magazine article, featuring him and Sarah Lamb. He hadn't made *The Inquirer*, but the piece in *Bizarro for Real* still pleased him. It included a fine picture of Bud on the cover. In the photo he stood by a rock wall, like in a cave. Sporting his khaki safari shirt and the widest grin I've ever seen on him, Bud held a can of Spam, Jalapeño flavor, in one hand and a flashlight in the other, pointing its beam to the side. There next to him, as if Bud's flashlight shone on her, they'd inserted a shot of Sarah Lamb on stage that night in Washington, D.C.

Sometimes, when he didn't think I was looking, I'd see Bud seething. Was he mad because he believed in *the steal*? Because he used to believe but knew better? Because Trump had lost? When

I congratulated him for not joining the criminals who broke into the Capitol building, he growled like an enraged grizzly.

MELANIE BROUGHT MEXICAN takeout to my place one night. I'd been thinking something over for the past month and raised the issue over cheese enchiladas and tacos.

"Melanie, would you consider working more hours with Bud and me?"

"What do you have in mind?"

"Our adventures with Jake Christian really spiced things up."

"And that spicy wife of his." She leaned over the kitchen table holding a taco, some of the cheese and little chunks of tomato falling onto her plate, as she took a bite.

"Hannah didn't sound happy, when I told her to forget Jake's life insurance and go for that lucrative divorce. I even tossed out the term, *spousal desertion.*"

"Very helpful of you, dear." Melanie kissed her finger tips and flicked them in the air. "Bye-bye, Hannah."

"My business pays the bills, but there's not enough challenge. I want to expand to missing persons cases."

"Great idea." Melanie swiped a paper napkin across her lips. "Bud could do the dangerous part."

"He'd like that," I said. "But he and I will do that together, like we did in Iraq."

"And I'll do the computer stuff."

"You could give up your second job. I could rent a better office."

"Crystal chandeliers and antique desks?"

"I'm thinking like two or three windows and a couple of cheap pictures on the wall."

"Nice."

CHAPTER 59

February-April 2021

At the office one day, Bud showed up around ten and plopped an envelope onto my desk. "I stopped off to see that slimy bitch. What's her name?"

Melanie looked up from her computer screen and supplied the answer: "Hannah."

"Right," Bud said. "You were gonna let Hannah off the hook, Stan, so I gave her a bill. You, me and Mel, we spent tons of billable hours out in nowhere-land working her case."

Crap. It was my job to bill clients. Of course, I hadn't done it in three months.

If Bud noticed my annoyance, he didn't let on. He backed away a few steps to give me space, and said, "The bitch blocked me in the doorway of her fancy house and gave me a fuck-off-Jack smirk." Bud raised the pitch of his voice, put a hand on his hip, wiggled his butt, and said, "'You assholes didn't finish the job. You didn't bring my husband home.'"

I couldn't help grinning at Bud's imitation. "We found him alive," I said. "That was all she asked." *But not what she wanted.*

Bud snorted. "Hannah didn't give a shit about that, and she wasn't about to pay. No problem. I told her I'd sue her husband

and his business for pain and suffering. My traumatic PSD, from being trapped down that well; that could flare up something fierce, if I had to testify. Unfortunate, but it would bankrupt her meal-ticket husband."

Inside the envelope I found a check from Sir Jacob Antiquities for $10,000 made out to S. Stein Investigations, signed by Sirjay Malik. Whatever annoyance I felt evaporated. "So, Hannah's talking to Malik. You think they—"

Bud corkscrewed his hand in the air. "That Indian prick is screwing her. Isn't everyone?"

I didn't believe that, not really. It didn't matter, though, did it? "Bud, I, I ..."

"Don't get all gooey with gratitude, partner," Bud said. "It was my pleasure."

OUR NEW ENTERPRISE began in March. Melanie sent out internet advertisements for our crack detective agency, and we solved two missing persons cases that month. We had two more in the works. I gave Melanie and Bud each $3,000 bonuses and leased a company car for Bud, a shiny red, used Prius. Melanie began looking for a nicer office, more Perry Mason and less Joe the termite eradicator.

The added income and a subsiding pandemic did us all good.

The election was well past, but our forced silence about Trump continued. I shared my frustration with Melanie night after night.

One day at the office, she sat us down at opposite sides of the table and said, "Here's what you two nerds are going to do."

I raised a hand to protest, but she stared me down. "It's all right to joke about Trump," she told me. "And you can tease about Biden," she said to Bud. "But you can't personally insult them." She looked from Bud to me, and continued. "If you want to say something serious, be cool about it."

"What if I just want to point out that Biden's an old SOB?" Bud asked.

"Drop the 'SOB' and keep it light, that's all. If you have doubts, write it down on paper and pass it back and forth like two eighth-graders." Melanie, like Mrs. Fitzgerald, my teacher back then, gave us each a stare-down.

I was tempted to mention that this would be easier with Trump exiled down in Florida. But what I said was, "Yes, Ma'am."

"You guys are going to be friends for a long time. I'm going to see to that."

AFTER THAT DISCUSSION, sitting around the office, I might insult Trump's hair-do. Bud would pitch in a comment about *Grandpa Joe Biden* falling down the steps of Air Force One. Melanie might offer a conjecture about what Vladimir Putin has on Trump. Bud would counter with, "Your nut-job stole the election."

Which could lead to, "Yours wanted to hang his own VP."

That could go on for a while. Our banter felt so good, I was tempted to hug Bud, but no one was vaccinated.

APRIL 2021

NEXT WEEK the vaccine will open up to everyone over sixteen. Melanie made reservations online for the two of us. Bud won't commit to a shot, even though his idol, our ex-president, admitted he got stuck.

Melanie regularly spends three weeknights and one weekend day at my place. Take-out food and intimate embraces abound. The rest of the time, she cares for her mother, sharing responsibility with her sister. Mel's sister sounds like a great gal, with a precocious daughter and a strong marriage. I'm going to meet the family next month, after we're all vaccinated. Then Melanie and I plan to get away for a few days at Lake Arrowhead.

I come home one day after work and find Melanie in a silky, soft-blue robe. She's tall, graceful and—what's the right word? —sleek? —elegant?

I unfasten the tie at the front of her robe, slip my hands inside and murmur, "You are magnificent."

She helps me off with my jacket. "You're the good looking one." She unbuttons my shirt and runs her hand over my chest.

I look into her lovely eyes. "I adore you, Melanie."

There, I've said it.

CHAPTER 60

BUD

AFTERWORD

I love Stan, but he's not as shrewd as he thinks. His name *is* on the business, but truth to tell, I'm the one with imagination. I was the guy doling out toilet paper last year, when the world went to shit. I'm the one who tracked Jake Christian to New Mexico. And I've scheduled my first Pfizer vaccination two days before Stan gets his. He imagines I'm anti-vax, and I don't deny it.

Drives him nuts.

Another thing that tweaks Stan; I won't answer when he asks if I still believe the election was stolen. Just between us, I'm not as damned sure as I was. Trump's zany lawyers threw out a few dozen theories about communist voting machines and stuff—some totally nuts, some possible, but possible for either side to have cheated that way. The commentators on Fox were all over each one of those theories, as if every piece of crap Rudy Giuliani threw out was fact.

Discourages the piss out of me.

I want to believe Trump. I do believe him, mostly. All those Biden votes, kept coming in late, after all. I also want to believe in our democracy. You can't believe Trump and believe in our elections at the same time. And what's America if our elections are bogus? As Stan reminded me, the world used to believe in the USA and our democracy. Not so much anymore. (He put that in a note, approved by Melanie. I refused to take the bait.)

There's my original theory too, the one about Trump doing the right thing. Then he sent thugs (patriots?) to the Capitol to attack his own vice president, and he didn't back them up like he promised. That whole mountain of manure pisses me off, so let's move on.

If you happen to be a *pro-gress-ive*, you probably think I'm the asshole. Okay, now look in the mirror. You have *issues* too.

Who's more sane here?

- *A tree-hugger who'd shut down industry to save rare chipmunks or a fuck-the-environment type who'll keep our factories spewing as California burns and hurricanes sweep Louisiana down the bayou? (Yeah, okay, global warming might actually be a thing.)*

- *A Robin Hood who taxes the rich to support the poor or a tycoon who lowers taxes for the rich to boost the economy and save American jobs?*

- *A leader who insults immigrants, locks them up, and ships them home or a politician offering them a bowl of soup, an Obama tee shirt and free health care?*

I used to think I knew all the answers. Silly me.

After all is said and done, Melanie's the smart one. She just got engaged to the most generous guy I know.

About the Author

Edward D. Webster's wide-ranging interests have led him to diverse careers; from teaching high school math to Navajo students in NM; to helping create an energy conservation program for a California county; to working to establish a center for abused, neglected and abandoned children.

Photo by: Patsy Wright

He is the author of an eclectic collection of books as well as articles appearing in publications as diverse as The *Boston Globe* and *Your Cat* magazine. His writing has been honored by groups ranging from the Colorado Independent Publishers Association and Midwest Book Review to the Boomer Times.

Ed admits to a fascination with unique, quirky, and bizarre human behavior. His acclaimed memoir, *A Year of Sundays (Taking the Plunge and our Cat to Explore Europe)* shares the eccentric tale of his months-long adventure in Europe with his spirited, blind wife and headstrong, deaf, geriatric cat.

In his historical novel, *Soul of Toledo*, about Spain in the 1440s, the diabolical nature of mankind stands out as madmen take over the city of Toledo and torture suspected Jews, thirty years before the Spanish Inquisition. (Based on a history by Benjamin Netanyahu's father.)

Webster also likes to mix unique characters to see what they'll do with/to each other. In his novel, *The Gentle Bomber's Melody,* a nutty woman, bearing a stolen baby, lands on the doorstep of a fugitive (but gentle) bomber hiding from the FBI. The result: irresistible insanity.

In his third novel, *Carlos Crosses the Line,* Webster cast his eye in other directions: the 1960s, the immigration quagmire, the validity of borders between people and countries—and most essentially, the question of what to believe if you don't accept your culture's traditional values.

Now, *American Nonsensical* crosses new lines, with a pair of charlatan preachers, multiple missing persons, a body (dead or alive?) in an old mining pit and two detectives seeking to solve the cases while arguing over Donald Trump and conspiracy theories. Here, Webster delves into the nature of truth, religion and sanity in an America churning with unprecedented tension.

Webster lives in Southern California with his divine wife and two amazing cats.

E. D. Webster's Website: www.edwardwebster.com
Facebook: www.facebook.com/edwebauthor
Twitter: @TheEdWebster
Instagram: TheEdWebster1

* 9 7 8 0 9 9 9 7 0 3 2 0 4 8 *